A.S. Byatt

VINTAGE **BYATT**

A. S. Byatt has written fourteen works of fiction—
Possession, which won the Booker Prize and the Irish
Times/Aer Lingus International Fiction Prize in
1990, as well as *The Shadow of the Sun*, *The Game*, *The
Virgin in the Garden*, *Still Life*, *Sugar and Other Stories*,
Angels & Insects, *The Matisse Stories*, *The Djinn in the
Nightingale's Eye*, *Babel Tower*, *Elementals*, *The Biogra-
pher's Tale*, *A Whistling Woman*, and *Little Black Book of
Stories*. Educated at Cambridge, she was a senior lec-
turer in English at University College London and a
distinguished critic and reviewer. Her critical work
includes *Degrees of Freedom: The Novels of Iris Murdoch*,
Unruly Times: Wordsworth and Coleridge, *Passions of the
Mind*, *Imagining Characters* (with Ignês Sodré), *On His-
tories and Stories*, and *Portraits in Fiction*. She lives in
London.

VINTAGE BYATT

A. S. Byatt

VINTAGE BOOKS

A Division of Random House, Inc.

New York

CONTENTS

VINTAGE BYATT

RACINE AND THE TABLECLOTH

When was it clear that Martha Crichton-Walker was the antagonist? Emily found this word for her much later, when she was a grown woman. How can a child, under-sized and fearful, have enough of a self to recognize an antagonist? She might imagine the malice of a cruel step-mother or a jealous sister, but not the clash of principle, the essential denial of an antagonist. She was too young to have thought-out beliefs. It was Miss Crichton-Walker's task, after all, to form and guide the unformed personality of Emily Bray. Emily Bray's ideas might have been thought to have been imparted by Martha Crichton-Walker, and this was in part the case, which made the recognition of antag-onism peculiarly difficult, certainly for Emily, possibly for both of them.

The first time Emily saw Miss Crichton-Walker in action was the first evening of her time at the school. The class was gathered together, in firelight and lamplight, round Miss Crichton-Walker's hearth, in her private sitting-room. Emily was the only new girl: she had arrived in mid-year, in exceptional circumstances (a family illness). The class were thirteen years old. There were twenty-eight of them, twenty-nine with Emily, a fact whose significance had not yet struck Emily. The fireside evening was Miss Crichton-Walker's way of noticing the death of a girl who had been in the class last term and had been struck by peritonitis after an operation on a burst appendix. This girl had been called Jan but had been known to the other girls as Hodgie. Did you hear about Hodgie, they all said to each other, rushing in with the news, mixing a kind of fear with a kind of glee, an undinted assurance of their own perpetuity. This was unfortunate for Emily; she felt like a substitute for Hodgie, although she was not. Miss Crichton-Walker gave them all pale cocoa and sugar-topped buns, and told them to sit on the floor round her. She spoke gently about their friend Hodgie whom they must all remember as she had been, full of life, sharing everything, a happy girl. She knew they were shocked; if at any later time they were to wish to bring any anxieties or regrets to her, she would be glad to share them. Regrets was an odd word, Emily perhaps noticed, though at that stage she was already willing enough to share Martha Crichton-Walker's tacit assumption that the girls would be bound to have regrets. Thirteen-year-old girls are unkind and in groups they are cruel.

There would have been regrets, however full of life and happy the lost Hodgie had been.

Miss Crichton-Walker told the girls a story. It made a peaceful scene, with the young faces turned up to the central storyteller, or down to the carpet. Emily Bray studied Miss Crichton-Walker's appearance, which was firmly benign and breastless. Rolled silver curls, almost like a barrister's wig, were aligned round a sweet face, very soft-skinned but nowhere slack, set mild. The eyes were wide and very blue, and the mouth had no droop, but was firm and even, straight-set. Lines led finely to it but did not carve any cavity or depression: they lay lightly, like a hairnet. Miss Crichton-Walker wore, on this occasion and almost always, a very fine woolen dress, nun's veiling with a pleated chest, long fitted sleeves, and a plain white Peter Pan collar. At her neck was a simple oval silver brooch. There was something essentially girlish—not skittish, or sullen, or liquid, but unmarked, about this face and body, which were also those of a neat, elderly woman.

The story was allegorical. It was about a caddis-grub which scuttled about on the floor of a pond, making itself a makeshift tube-house of bits of gravel, twigs and weed to cover its vulnerable and ugly little grub body. Its movements were awkward and painful, its world dank and dimly lit. One day it was seized with an urge to climb which it could not ignore. Painfully it drew its squashy length out of its abandoned house and made its way, bursting and anguished, up a tall bulrush. In the bright outer air it hardened, cased in, and then most painfully burst and split, issuing forth with fine iridescent wings and darting movements, a creature of light and air. Miss Crichton-Walker enjoyed this tale of contrasts. Emily Bray could not make out—she was never much to make out, it was her failing—what the other girls thought or felt. Always afterwards she imagined the dead Hodgie as grub-like and squashy. During the telling she imagined the others as little girls, although she herself was the smallest in size, puny and stick-like. They all sat in their dressing-gowns and pyjamas, washed and shapeless. Later in the dormitory they would chatter agitatedly, full of opinions and feelings, pointing fingers, jutting chins. Here they were secret and docile. Miss Crichton-Walker told them they had had a peaceful evening together and that had been good. Emily Bray saw that there were two outsiders in the room. There was herself, set aside from the emotion that was swimming around, and there was Miss Crichton-Walker who wanted them all to be sharing something.

Every Wednesday and every Sunday the school walked into the centre of the cathedral city to go to church. On Wednesday they had their own service, shared with their brother school, Holy Communion and Morning Prayer. On Sunday they made part—a large part—of the general congregation. There were rules about walking through the city; they did not go in a crocodile, but were strictly forbidden to walk more than two abreast through the narrow streets. Three laughing girls, horseplaying perhaps, had once swept over an old lady outside Boot's, had fractured frail bones and been cautioned by the Police. A result of this reasonable ruling was that it was important for each girl to have a partner, someone to walk with, a best friend. Girls of that age choose best friends naturally, or so Emily had observed, who had not had a best friend since her days in the junior school, before her unfortunate habits became pronounced. The church-walking added forms and rituals to the selection and rejection of best friends. Everyone knew if a couple split up, or a new couple was formed. Emily discovered quickly enough that there was a floating population of rejects, ragtag, bobtail, who formed feebler ties, *ad hoc* partnerships, with half an eye on the chance of a rift between a more acceptable pairing. She assumed she would belong with these. She had no illusions about her chances of popularity in the class. The best she could hope for was decent anonymity. She also knew that decent anonymity was unlikely. When the exam results came, she would be found out. In the interim, she realised quickly enough the significance of the size of the class, twenty-nine girls. There would always be a final reject, one running round when all the musical chairs were occupied. That one would be Emily Bray.

You might suppose that grown-up, intelligent school-mistresses would be capable of seeing the significance of twenty-nine, or that it might be possible for Emily to point it out, or recall it to them, if they did not. You also almost certainly know enough about conventional institutional rigours to be unsurprised that it was quite impossible for Emily to say anything coherent when, as happened regularly, she was caught up in the street and reprimanded for tagging along in a threesome. (Walking anywhere alone was an unthinkable and serious offense.) She dreaded Wednesdays and Sundays, working herself up on Tuesdays and Saturdays to beg, with mortified mock-casual misery, to be allowed to come along. After she began to get exam results, the situation, as she had foreseen, worsened. With appalling regularity, with unnatural ease and insulting catholicity, Emily Bray came first in almost everything except maths and domestic science. She came first in the theoretical paper of domestic science, but her handiwork let her down. She was a simply intellectual creature. She was physically undeveloped, no good at sport, no one to chatter to about sex, or *schwärmerei*, delicious shoes or pony club confrontations. She had an image of herself in their minds as a kind of abacus in its limited frame, clicking mnemonics, solving problems, recording transactions. She waited to be disliked and they duly disliked her. There were clever girls, Flora Marsh for example, who were not so disliked: Flora was peaceably beautiful, big and slender and athletic and wholesome, genuinely modest, wanting to be mother of six and live in the country. Flora had a horse and a church partner, Catherine, she had known since she was five.

Flora's handwriting was even and generous, flowing on in blue running curves and rhythmic spaces. Emily Bray wrote hunched over the page, jabbing at it with a weak-nibbed fountain pen. There was never a misspelled word, but the whole was blotted and a little smeared and grimy, the lines uneven, the characters without settled forms. In Emily's second year Miss Crichton-Walker addressed their class on its work and said in front of all of them that it was her habit always to read the best set of exam papers. In this case that was, as they all knew, Emily Bray's but she was afraid that she had had to return these unfinished since she was distressed by the aggressive handwriting. The papers were a disgrace in other ways too, nastily presented, and dirty. If Emily would be kind enough to make a fair copy she would be delighted to read them. She delivered this judgment, as was her habit, with a slight smile, not depre-cating, not mitigating, but pleased and admiring. Admiring the accuracy of her own expressions, or pleased with the placing of the barb? It did not occur to young Emily to ask herself that question, though she noted and remembered the smile accurately enough to answer it, when she was ready, when her account was made up. But the child did not know what judgment the woman would make, or indeed that the woman would judge. The child believed she was shrugging off the judgment of herself. Of course the paper was dirty: schools thought dirt mattered; she believed it did not. She opposed herself like a shut sea anemone, a wall of muscle, a tight sphincter. It is also true, changing the metaphor, that the judgment dropped in heavily and fast, like a stone into a pond, to rest unshifted on the bottom.

She noted the word, aggressive, as on that earlier occasion she had noted "regrets." She remembered writing those speedy, spattered pages—an essay on Hamlet's delays, a character-analysis of Emma Woodhouse. She had written for pleasure. She had written for an imaginary ideal Reader, perfectly aware of her own strengths and failings, her approximations to proper judgments, her flashes of understanding. If she had thought for ten minutes she would have known that no such Reader existed, there was only Miss Harvey and beyond Miss Harvey Miss Crichton-Walker. But she never yielded those ten minutes. If the real Reader did not exist it was necessary to invent Him, and Emily did so. The pronoun is an accurate rendering of Emily's vaguest intimation of his nature. In a female institution where justice, or judgment, was Miss Crichton-Walker, benign impartiality seemed to be male. Emily did not associate the Reader with the gods worshipped in the cathedral on Sundays. God the Judge and God the Friend and God the rushing wind of the Spirit were familiars of Miss Crichton-Walker invoked with an effort of ecstasy in evening prayers in the school, put together with music and branched stone and beautiful words and a sighing sentiment in the choir stalls. Emily could not reasonably see why the propensity to believe this myth should have any primary guarantee of touching at truth, any more than the propensity to believe

Apollo, or Odin, or Gautama Buddha, or Mithras. She was not aware that she believed in the Reader, though as she got older she became more precise and firm about his attributes. He was dry and clear, he was all-knowing but not messily infinite. He kept his proportion and his place. He had no face and no imaginary arms to enfold or heart to beat: his nature was not love, but understanding. Invoked, as the black ink spattered in the smell of chalk dust and dirty fingers, he brought with him a foreign air, sun-baked on sand, sterile, heady, tolerably hot. It is not too much to say that in those seemingly endless years in that place Emily was enabled to continue because she was able to go on believing in the Reader.

She did not make a fair copy of her papers for Miss Crichton-Walker. She believed that it was not really expected of her, that the point to be made had been made. Here she may have been doing Miss Crichton-Walker an injustice, though this is doubtful. Miss Crichton-Walker was expert in morals, not in *Hamlet* or *Emma*.

When she was fifteen Emily devised a way of dealing with the church walk. The city was medieval still in many parts, and, more particularly, was surrounded with long stretches of city wall, with honey-pale stone battlements, inside which two people could walk side by side, looking out over the cathedral close and the twisting lanes, away down to the surrounding plain. She discovered that if she ducked back behind the church, under an arched gateway, she could, if she went briskly, walk back along the ramparts almost all the way, out-flanking the mainstream of female pairs, descending only for the last few hundred yards, where it was possible to dodge through back streets to where the school stood, in its pleasant gardens, inside its own lesser barbed wall. No one who has not been an inmate can know exactly how powerful is the hunger for solitude which grows in the constant company, day and night, feeding, washing, learning, sleeping, almost even, with partition walls on tubular metal stems, excreting. It is said women make bad prisoners because they are not by nature communal creatures. Emily thought about these things in the snatched breathing spaces she had made on the high walls, but thought of the need of solitude as hers only, over against the crushing others, though they must all also, she later recognized, have had their inner lives, their reticences, their inexpressive needs. She thought things out on that wall, French grammar and Euclid, the existence of males, somewhere else, the purpose of her life. She grew bold and regular—there was a particular tree, a self-planted willow, whose catkins she returned to each week, tight dark reddish buds, bursting silvery grey, a week damp and glossy grey fur and then the full pussy willow, softly bristling, powdered with bright yellow in the blue. One day when she was standing looking at these vegetable lights Miss Crichton-Walker and another figure appeared to materialize in front of her, side by stiff side. They must have come up one of the flights of steps from the grass bank inside the wall, now bright with daffodils and crocus; Emily remembered them appearing head-first, as though rising from the ground, rather than walking towards her. Miss Crichton-Walker had a grey woollen coat with a curly lambskin collar in a darker pewter; on her head was a matching hat, a cylinder of curly fur. There were two rows of buttons on her chest; she wore grey kid gloves and sensible shoes, laced and rigorous. She stood there for a moment on the wall and saw Emily Bray by her willow tree. There was no question in Emily's mind that they had stared at each other, silently. Then Miss Crichton-Walker pointed over the parapet, indicating some cloud formation to her companion, of whose identity Emily formed no impression at all, and they passed on, in complete silence. She even wondered wildly, as she hurried away back towards the school, if she had not seen them at all.

She had, of course. Miss Crichton-Walker waited until evening prayers to announce, in front of the school, that she wanted to see Emily Bray, tomorrow after lunch, thus leaving Emily all night and half a day to wonder what would be said or done. It was a school without formal punishments. No one wrote lines, or sat through detentions, or penitently scrubbed washroom floors. And yet everyone, not only Emily Bray, was afraid of committing a fault before Miss Crichton-Walker. She could make you feel a real worm, the girls said, the lowest of the low, for having illegal runny honey instead of permitted hard honey, for running across the tennis lawns in heavy shoes, for smiling at boys. What she could do to those who cheated or stole or bullied was

less clear and less urgent. On the whole they didn't. They
were on the whole nice girls. They accepted Miss Crichton-
Walker's judgment of them, and this was their heavy
punishment.

Emily stood in front of Miss Crichton-Walker in her study.
Between their faces was a silver rose bowl, full of spring
flowers. Miss Crichton-Walker was small and straight in
a large upright armchair. She asked Emily what she had
been doing on the wall, and Emily said that she had no one
to walk home from church with, so came that way. She
thought of adding, most girls of my age, in reasonable day
schools, can walk alone in a city in the middle of the morning, quite naturally, anybody might. Miss Crichton-Walker
said that Emily was arrogant and unsociable, had made little or no effort to fit in with the community ever since she
came, appeared to think that the world was made for her
convenience. She set herself against everything, Miss
Crichton-Walker said, she was positively depraved. Here
was another word to add to those others, regrets, aggressive,
depraved. Emily said afterwards to Flora Marsh, who asked
what had happened, that Miss Crichton-Walker had told
her that she was depraved. Surely not, said Flora, and, yes
she did, said Emily, she did, that is what she *thinks*. You
may have your own views about whether Miss Crichton-
Walker could in sober fact have uttered the word depraved,
in her soft, silvery voice, to an awkward girl who had tried
to walk alone in mid-morning, to look at a pussy willow,

to think. It may be that Emily invented the word herself, saying it for bravado to Flora Marsh after the event, though I would then argue, in defence of Emily, that the word must have been in the air during that dialogue for her to pick up, the feeling was there, Miss Crichton-Walker sensed her solitude as something corrupt, contaminating, depraved. What was to be done? For the next four weeks, Miss Crichton-Walker said, she would walk back from church with Emily herself. It was clear that she found this prospect as disagreeable as Emily possibly could. She was punishing both of them.

What could they say to each other, the awkward pair, one shuffling downcast, one with a regular inhibited stride? Emily did not regard it as her place to initiate any conversation: she believed any approach would have been unacceptable, and may well have been right. You will think that Miss Crichton-Walker might have taken the opportunity to draw Emily out, to find out why she was unhappy, or what she thought of her education. She did say some things that might have been thought to be part of such a conversation, though she said them reluctantly, in a repressed, husky voice, as though they were hard to bring out. She was content for much the larger part of their four weeks' perambulation to say nothing at all, pacing it out like prison exercise, a regular rhythmic pavement-tapping with which Emily was compelled to try to keep time. Occasionally spontaneous remarks broke from her, not in the strained, clutching voice of her confidential manner, but with a sharp, clear ring. These were remarks about Emily's personal appearance for which she felt—it is not too strong a word, though this time it is mine, or Emily's; Martha Crichton-Walker is innocent of uttering it—she felt disgust. "For the second week running you have a grey line round your neck, Emily, like the scum you deposit round the rim of the bath." "You have a poor skin, Emily. Ask Sister to give those blackheads some attention: you must have an abnormal concentration of grease in your nasal area, or else you are unusually skimpy in your attention to your personal hygiene. Have you tried medicated soap?" "Your hair is lank, Emily. I do not like to think of the probable state of your hatband." "May I see your hands? I have never understood how people can bring themselves to bite their nails. How unpleasant and profitless to chew away one's own flesh in this manner. I see you are imbued with ink as some people are dyed with nicotine: it is just as disagreeable. Perhaps the state of your hands goes some way to explain your very poor presentation of your work: you seem to *wallow* in ink to a quite unusual extent. Please purchase a pumice stone and a lemon and scour it away before we go out next week. Please borrow a knife from the kitchen and prise away the boot-polished mud from your shoe-heels—that is a lazy way of going on that does not deceive the eye, and increases the impression of slovenliness."

None of these remarks was wholly unjust, though the

number of them, the ingenuity with which they were elaborated and dilated on, were perhaps excessive? Emily imagined the little nose sniffing at the armpits of her discarded vests, at the stains on her pants. She sweated with anxiety inside her serge overcoat, waiting outside Miss Crichton-Walker's study, and imagined Miss Crichton-Walker could smell her fear rising out of the wool, running down her lisle stockings. Miss Crichton-Walker seemed to be without natural exudations. A whiff of lavender, a hint of mothball.

She talked to Emily about her family. Emily's family do not come into this story, though you may perhaps be wondering about them, you might need at least to know whether the authority they represented would be likely to reinforce that of Miss Crichton-Walker, or to present some counter-balance, some other form of moral priority. Emily Bray was a scholarship girl, from a large Potteries family of five children. Emily's father was a foreman in charge of a kiln which fired a curious mixture of teacups thick with lilies of the valley, dinner plates edged severely with gold dagger-shapes, and virulently green pottery dogs with gaping mouths to hold toothbrushes or rubber bands. Emily's mother had, until her marriage, been an elementary school teacher, trained in Homerton in Cambridge, where she had developed the aspiration to send her sons and daughters to that university. Emily was the eldest of the five children; the next one, Martin, was a mongol. Emily's mother considered Martin a condign punishment of her aspirations to betterment. She loved him extravagantly and best. The three younger ones were left to their own resources, much of the time. Emily felt for them, and their cramped, busy, noisy little life, some of the distaste Miss Crichton-Walker felt for her, perhaps for all the girls. There are two things to note in this brief summing-up—a hereditary propensity to feel guilty, handed down to Emily from her briefly ambitious mother, and the existence of Martin.

Miss Crichton-Walker knew about Martin, of course. He had been part of the argument for Emily's scholarship, awarded on grounds of social need, in line with the principles of the school, rather than academic merit. Miss Crichton-Walker, in so far as she wanted to talk to Emily at all, wanted to talk about Martin. Tell me about your brothers and sisters, dear, she said, and Emily listed them, Martin, thirteen, Lorna, ten, Gareth, eight, Amanda, five. Did she miss them, said Miss Crichton-Walker, and Emily said no, not really, she saw them in the holidays, they were very noisy, if she was working. But you must love them, said Miss Crichton-Walker, in her choking voice, you must feel you are, hmm, not properly part of their lives? Emily did indeed feel excluded from the bustle of the kitchen, and more confusedly, more anxiously, from her mother's love, by Martin. But she sensed, rightly, that Miss Crichton-Walker wished her to feel cut off by the privilege of being at the school, guilty of not offering the help she might have done. She described teaching Amanda to read, in two weeks flat, and Miss Crichton-Walker said she noticed

Emily did not mention Martin. Was that because she was embarrassed, or because she felt badly about him? She must never be embarrassed by Martin's misfortune, said Miss Crichton-Walker, who was embarrassed by Emily's inkstains and shoe-mud most sincerely, she must acknowledge her own. I do love him, said Emily, who did, who had nursed and sung to him, when he was smaller, who suffered from his crashing forays into her half-bedroom, from scribbled-on exercises, bath-drowned books. She remembered his heavy amiable twinkle. We all love him, she said. You must try to do so, said Miss Crichton-Walker.

Miss Crichton-Walker had her lighter moments. Some of these were part of the school's traditional pattern, in which she had her traditional place, such as the telling of the school ghost story at Hallowe'en, a firelit occasion for everyone, in the stark dining-room, by the light of two hundred candles inside the grinning orange skins of two hundred swedes. The girls sat for hours hollowing out these heads, at first nibbling the sweet vegetable, then revolted by it. For days afterwards the school smelled like a byre: during the storytelling the roasting smell of singed turnip overlay the persisting smell of the raw scrapings. For an hour before the storytelling they had their annual time of licence, running screaming through the dark garden, in sheets and knitted spiderwebs, jointed paper skeletons and floating batwings. The ghost story concerned an improb-able encounter between a Roman centurion and a phan-

tom cow in a venerable clump of trees in the centre of
which stood an old and magnificent swing. Anyone meeting the white cow would vanish, the story ran, as in some
other time the centurion had vanished, though imperfectly,
leaving traces of his presence among the trees, the glimpsed
sheen on a helmet, the flutter of his leather skirting. There
was always a lot of suppressed giggling during Miss Crichton-Walker's rendering of this tale, which, to tell the truth,
lacked narrative tension and a conclusive climax. The giggling was because of the proliferate embroidered legends
which were in everyone's mind of Miss Crichton-Walker's
secret, nocturnal, naked swinging in that clump of trees.
She had once very determinedly, in Emily's presence, told
a group of the girls that she enjoyed sitting naked in her
room, on the hearth by the fire in the evening. It is very
pleasant to feel the air on your skin, said Miss Crichton-
Walker, holding her hands judicially before her chest, fin-
gertips touching. It is natural and pleasant. Emily did not
know what authority there was for the legend that she
swung naked at night in the garden. She had perhaps once
told such a group of girls that she would *like* to do so, that
it would be good and pleasant to swoop unencumbered
through the dark air, to touch the lowest branches of the
thick trees with naked toes, to feel the cool rush along her
body. There were in any case now several stories of her
having been solidly seen doing just that, urging herself to
and fro, milky-white in the dark. This image, with its
moon face and rigid imperturbable curls, was much more

vivid in Emily's mind at Hallowe'en than any ghostly cow or centurion. The swing, in its wooden authority and weight, reminded Emily of a gibbet. The storytelling, more vaguely, reminded her of the first evening and the allegorizing of Hodgie's death.

Their first stirrings of appetite and anxiety, directed at the only vaguely differentiated mass of the brother school's congregation, aroused considerable efforts of repressive energy in Miss Crichton-Walker. It was said that under a previous, more liberal headmistress, the boys had been encouraged to walk the girls back from church. No one would even have dared to propose this to her. That there were girls who flouted this prohibition Emily knew, though only by remote hearsay. She could not tell one boy from another and was in love with Benedick, with Pierre, with Max Ravenscar, with Mr. Knightly. There was an annual school dance, to which the boys were brought in silent, damp-palmed, hunched clumps in two or three buses. Miss Crichton-Walker could not prevent this dance: it was an ancient tradition: the boys' headmaster and the governors liked it to exist as a sign of educational liberality. But she spoke against it. For weeks before the arrival of the boys she spent her little Saturday evening homilies on warning the girls. It was not clear, from what she said, exactly what she was warning against. She was famous in the Lower Sixth for having managed explicitly to say that if any boy pressed too close, held any girl too tightly, that girl must say composedly "Shall we sit this one out?" Girls rolled on their dormitory beds gasping out this *mot* in bursts of wild laughter and tones of accomplishment parody. (The school was full of accomplished parodists of Miss Crichton-Walker.) They polished their coloured court shoes, scarlet and peacock, and fingered the stiff taffeta folds of their huge skirts, which they wore with demure and provocative silk shirts and tightly-pulled wide belts. In later years Emily remembered as the centre of Miss Crichton-Walker's attack on sexual promptings, on the possibilities of arousal, a curiously elaborate disquisition on the unpleasantness and unnatural function of the female razor. She could not bring herself to mention the armpits. She spoke at length, with an access of clarity and precision, about the evil effects on the skin of frequent shaving of the legs, which left "as I know very well, an unsightly dark stubble, which then has to be treated more and more frequently, once you have shaved away the first natural soft down. Any gardener will tell you that grass grows coarser after it has once been cut. I ask all the girls who have razors in the school to send them home, please, and all girls to ask their parents not to send such things through the post." It was also during the weeks preceding the dance that she spoke against deodorants, saying that they were unnecessary for young girls and that the effects of prolonged chemical treatment of delicate skin were not yet known. A little talcum powder would be quite sufficient if they feared becoming heated.

I am not going to describe the dance, which was sad for

almost all of them, must have been, as they stood in their resolutely unmingled ranks on either side of the grey school hall. Nothing of interest really happened to Emily on that occasion, as she must, in her secret mind, have known it would not. It faded rapidly enough in her memory, whereas Miss Crichton-Walker's peculiar anxiety about it, even down to her curious analogy between razors and lawn-mowers, remained stamped there, clear and pungent, an odd and significant trace of the days of her education. In due course this memory accrued to itself Emily's later reflections on the punning names of depilatories, all of which aroused in her mind a trace-image of Miss Crichton-Walker's swinging, white, hairless body in the moonlight. Veet. Immac. Nair. Emily at the time of the static dance was beginning to sample the pleasures of being a linguist. Nair sounded like a Miltonic coinage for Satanic scaliness. Veet was a thick English version of French rapidity and discreet efficiency. Immac, in the connexion of Miss Crichton-Walker, was particularly satisfying, carrying with it the Latin, maculata, stained or spotted, immaculata, unstained, unspotted, and the Immaculata Conception, which, Emily was taught at this time, referred to the stainless or spotless begetting of the Virgin herself, not to the subsequent self-contained, unpunctured, manless begetting of the Son. The girls in the dormitories were roused by Miss Crichton-Walker to swap anecdotes about Veet, which according to them had "the—most—terrible—*smell*" and produced a stinking slop of hairy grease. No one sent her razor home. It was generally agreed that Miss Crichton-Walker had too little bodily hair to know what it was to worry about it.

Meanwhile, and at the same time, there was Racine. You may be amused that Miss Crichton-Walker should simultaneously ban ladies' razors and promote the study of *Phèdre*. It is amusing. It is amusing that the same girls should already have been exposed to the betrayed and betraying cries of Ophelia's madness. "Then up he rose, and doffed his clothes, and dupped the chamber door. Let in the maid that out a maid, never departed more." It is the word "dupped" that is so upsetting in that little song, perhaps because it recalls another Shakespearean word that rhymes with it, Iago's black ram tupping the white ewe, Desdemona. Get thee to a nunnery, said Hamlet, and there was Emily, in a nunnery, never out of one, in a rustle of terrible words and delicate and gross suggestions, the stuff of her studies. But that is not what I wanted to say about Racine. Shakespeare came upon Emily gradually, she could accommodate him, he had always been there. Racine was sudden and new. That is not it, either, not what I wanted to say.

Think of it. Twenty girls or so—were there so many?— in the A-level French class, and in front of each a similar, if not identical, small, slim greenish book, more or less used, more or less stained. When they riffled through the pages, the text did not look attractive. It proceeded in strict, soldierly columns of rhymed couplets, a form disliked by both the poetry-lovers and the indifferent amongst them.

Nothing seemed to be happening, it all seemed to be the same. The speeches were very long. There appeared to be no interchange, no battle of dialogue, no action. *Phèdre*. The French teacher told them that the play was based on the *Hippolytus* of Euripides, and that Racine had altered the plot by adding a character, a young girl, Aricie, whom Hippolytus should fall in love with. She neglected to describe the original play, which they did not know. They wrote down, Hippolytus, Euripides, Aricie. She told them that the play kept the unities of classical drama, and told them what these unities were, and they wrote them down. The Unity of Time = One Day. The Unity of Space = One Place. The Unity of Action = One Plot. She neglected to say what kind of effect these constrictions might have on an imagined world: she offered a half-hearted rationale she clearly despised a little herself, as though the Greeks and the French were children who made unnecessary rules for themselves, did not see wider horizons. The girls were embarrassed by having to read this passionate sing-song verse aloud in French. Emily shared their initial reluctance, their near-apathy. She was later to believe that only she became a secret addict of Racine's convoluted world, tortuously lucid, savage and controlled. As I said, the imagination of the other girls' thoughts was not Emily's strength. In Racine's world, all the inmates were gripped wholly by incompatible passions which swelled uncontrollably to fill their whole universe, brimming over and drowning its horizons. They were all creatures of excess, their secret blood burned and boiled and an unimaginably hot bright sun glared down in judgment. They were all horribly and beautifully interwoven, tearing each other apart in a perfectly choreographed dance, every move inevitable, lovely, destroying. In this world men and women had high and terrible fates which were themselves and yet greater than themselves. Phèdre's love for Hippolyte was wholly unnatural, dragging her world askew, wholly inevitable, a force like a flood, or a conflagration, or an eruption. This art described a world of monstrous disorder and excess and at the same time ordered it with iron control and constrictions, the closed world of the classical stage and the prescribed dialogue, the flexible, shining, inescapable steel mesh of that regular, regulated singing verse. It was a world in which the artist was in unusual collusion with the Reader, his art like a mapping trellis between the voyeur and the terrible writhing of the characters. It was an austere and adult art, Emily thought, who knew little about adults, only that they were unlike Miss Crichton-Walker, and had anxieties other than those of her tired and over-stretched mother. The Reader was adult. The Reader saw with the pitiless clarity of Racine—and also with Racine's impersonal sympathy—just how far human beings could go, what they were capable of.

After the April foolery, Miss Crichton-Walker said she would not have believed the girls were capable of it. No one, no one Emily knew at least, knew how the folly had started. It was "passed on," in giggled injunctions, returning again embroidered to earlier tellers. It must have originated with some pair, or pairs, of boys and girls who had managed to make contact at the static dance, who had perhaps sat a few waltzes out together, as Miss Crichton-Walker had bidden. The instruction they all received was that on Sunday April 1st the boys were to sit on the girls' side of the church and vice versa. Not to mingle, that is. To change places *en bloc*, from the bride's side to the bridegroom's. No rationale was given for this jape, which was immediately perceived by all the girls and boys involved as exquisitely funny, a kind of epitome of disorder and misrule. The bolder spirits took care to arrive early, and arrange themselves decorously in their contrary pews. The others followed like meek sheep. To show that they were not mocking God, the whole congregation then worshipped with almost unnatural fervour and devotion, chanting the responses, not wriggling or shifting in their seats. The Vicar raised his eyebrows, smiled benignly, and conducted the service with no reference to the change.

Miss Crichton-Walker was shocked, or hurt, to the quick. It was as though, Emily thought very much later, some kind of ritual travesty had happened, the Dionysiac preparing of Pentheus, in his women's skirts, for the maenads to feast on. Though this analogy is misleading: Miss Crichton-Walker's anguish was a kind of puritanical modesty. What outraged her was that, as she saw it, she, and the institution of which she was the head, had been irrevocably shamed in front of the enemy. In the icy little speech she made to the school at the next breakfast she did not mention any insult to the church, Emily was almost sure. Nor did she dart barbs of precise, disgusted speech at the assembled girls: she was too upset for that. Uncharacteristically she wavered, beginning "Something has happened . . . something has taken place . . . you will all know what I am speaking of . . ." gathering strength only when she came to her proposed expiation of the sin. "Because of what you have done," she said, "I shall stand here, without food, during all today's meals. I shall eat nothing. You can watch me while you eat, and think about what you have done."

Did they? Emily's uncertainty about the thoughts of the others held for this extraordinary act of vicarious penance, too. Did they laugh about it? Were they shocked and anxious? Through all three meals of the day they ate in silence, forks clattering vigorously on plates, iron spoons scraping metal trays, amongst the smell of browned shepherd's pie and institutional custard, whilst that little figure stood, doll-like, absurd and compelling, her fine lips pursed, her judicial curls regular round her motionless cheeks. Emily herself, as always, she came to understand, reacted with a fatal doubleness. She *thought* Miss Crichton-Walker was behaving in an undignified and disproportionate manner. She *felt*, gloomily and heavily, that she had indeed greatly damaged Miss Crichton-Walker, had done her a great and now inexpiable wrong, for which Miss Crichton-Walker was busily heaping coals of fire on her uncomprehending but guilty head. Miss Crichton-Walker was atoning for Emily's sin, which Emily had not, until then, known to be a sin. Emily was trapped.

When the A-level exams came, Emily developed a personality, not perhaps, you will think, a very agreeable one. She was approaching a time when her skills would be publicly measured and valued, or so she thought, as she became increasingly aware that they were positively deplored, not only by the other girls, but by Miss Crichton-Walker. The school was academically sound but made it a matter of principle not to put much emphasis on these matters, to encourage leadership, community spirit, charity, usefulness and other worthy undertakings. Girls went to university but were not excessively, not even much praised for this. Nevertheless, Emily knew it was there. At the end of the tunnel—which she visualized, since one must never allow a metaphor to lie dead and inert, as some kind of curving, tough, skinny tube in which she was confined and struggling, seeing the outside world dimly and distorted—at the end of the tunnel there was, there must be, light and a rational world full of aspiring Readers. She prepared for the A level with a desperate chastity of effort, as a nun might prepare for her vows. She learned to write neatly, overnight it seemed, so that no one recognized these new, confident, precisely black unblotted lines. She developed a pugnacious tilt to her chin. Someone in her form took her by the ears and banged her head repeatedly on the classroom wall, crying out "you don't even have to try, you smug little bitch . . ." but this was not true. She struggled secretly for perfection. She read four more of Racine's plays, feverishly sure that she would, when the time came, write something inadequate, ill-informed about his range, his beliefs, his wisdom. As I write, I can feel you judging her adversely, thinking, what a to-do, or even, smug little bitch. If I had set out to write a story about someone trying for perfection as a high diver, perhaps, or as a long distance runner, or even as a pianist, I should not so have lost your sympathy at this point. I could have been sure of exciting you with heavy muscles going up the concrete steps for the twentieth or thirtieth time, with the smooth sheet of aquamarine always waiting, the rush of white air, white air in water, the drum in the eardrums, the conversion of flesh and bone to a perfect parabola. You would have understood this in terms of some great effort of your own, at some time, as I now take plea-sure in understanding the work of televised snooker players, thinking a series of curves and lines and then making these real, watching the balls dart and clatter and fall into beautiful shapes, as I also take pleasure in the skill of the cameramen, who can show my ignorant eye, picking out this detail and that, where the beautiful lines lie, where there are impossi-bilities in the way, where the danger is, and where success.

Maybe I am wrong in supposing that there is something inherently distasteful in the struggles of the solitary clever child. Or maybe the reason is not that cleverness—academic cleverness—is distasteful, but that writing about it is *déjà-vu*, wearisome. That's what they all become, solitary clever children, complaining writers, misunderstood. Not Emily. She did not become a writer, about her misunderstood cleverness or anything else.

Maybe you are not unsympathetic at all, and I have now made you so. You can do without a paranoid narrator. Back to Miss Crichton-Walker, always in wait.

On the evening before the first exam, Miss Crichton-Walker addressed to the whole school one of her little homilies. It was summer, and she wore a silvery grey dress, with her small silver brooch. In front of her was a plain silver bowl of flowers—pink roses, blue irises, something white and lacy and delicate surrounding them. The exams, she told the school, were due to begin tomorrow, and she hoped the junior girls would remember to keep quiet and not to shout under the hall windows whilst others were writing. There were girls in the school, she said, who appeared to attach a great deal of importance to exam results. Who seemed to think that there was some kind of exceptional merit in doing well. She hoped she had never allowed the school to suppose that her own values were wrapped up in this kind of achievement. Everything they did mattered, mattered very much, everything was of extreme importance in its own way. She herself, she said, had written books, and she had embroidered tablecloths. She would not say that there was not as much lasting value, as much pleasure for others, in a well-made tablecloth as in a well-written book.

While she talked, her eyes appeared to meet Emily's, steely and intimate. Any good speaker can do this, can appear to single out one or another of the listeners, can give the illusion that all are personally addressed. Miss Crichton-Walker was not a good speaker, normally: her voice was always choked with emotion, which she was not so much sharing as desperately offering to the stony, the uncaring of her imagination. She expected to be misunderstood, even in gaudier moments to be reviled, though persisting. Emily understood this without knowing how she knew it, or even that she knew it. But on this one occasion she knew with equal certainty that Miss Crichton-Walker's words were for her, that they were delivered with a sweet animus, an absolute antagonism into which Miss Crichton-Walker's whole cramped self was momentarily directed. At first she stared back angrily, her little chin grimly up, and thought that Miss Crichton-Walker was exceedingly vulgar, that what mattered was not exam results, God save the mark, but *Racine*. And then, in a spirit of almost academic justice, she tried to think of the virtue of tablecloths, and thought of her own Auntie Florence, in fact a great-aunt. And, after a moment or two, twisted her head, broke the locked gaze, looked down at the parquet.

In the Potteries, she had many great-aunts. Auntie Annie, Auntie Ada, Auntie Miriam, Auntie Gertrude, Auntie Florence. Auntie Florence was the eldest and had been the most beautiful. She had always looked after her mother, in

pinched circumstances, and had married late, having no
children of her own, though always, Emily's mother said,
much in demand to look after other people's. Her mother
had died when Florrie was fifty-four, demented and senile.
Her husband had had a stroke, that year, and had lain help-
lessly in bed for the next ten, fed and tended by Auntie
Florrie. She had had, in her youth, long golden hair, so
long she could sit on it. She had always wanted to travel
abroad, Auntie Florrie, whose education had ceased formally
at fourteen, who read Dickens and Trollope, Dumas and
Harriet Beecher Stowe. When Uncle Ted died at last, Aunt
Florrie had a little money and thought she might travel.
But then Auntie Miriam sickened, went off her feet, trembled uncontrollably and Florrie was called in by her children, busy with their own children. She was the one who
was available, like, Emily's mother said. She had always
been as strong as a horse, toiling up and down them stairs,
fetching and carrying for Gran, for Uncle Ted, and then
for poor Miriam. She always looked so wholesome and
ready for anything. But she was seventy-two when Miriam
died and arthritis got her. She couldn't go very far. She
went on with the embroidery she'd always done, beautiful
work of all kinds, bouquets and arabesques and trellises of
flowers in jeweled colours on white linen, or in white silk
on white pillowcases, or in rainbow colours and patterns
from every century, Renaissance, Classical, Victorian, Art
Nouveau, on satin cushion covers. If you went to see her
you took her a present of white satin to work on. She liked

heavy bridal satin best. She liked the creamy whites and could never take to the new glaring whites in the nylon satins. When she was eighty-five the local paper had an article in it about her marvellous work, and a photograph of Auntie Florrie in her little sitting-room, sitting upright amongst all the white rectangles of her needlework, draped on all the furniture. Aunt Florrie still wore a woven crown of her own thinning hair. She had a good neighbour, Emily's mother said, who came in and did it for her. She couldn't do much work, now, though. The arthritis had got her hands.

After Miss Crichton-Walker's little talk, Emily began to cry. For the first half-hour of the crying she herself thought that it was just a nervous reaction, a kind of irritation, because she was so strung-up for the next day's examination, and that it would soon stop. She cried at first rather noisily in a subterranean locker-room, swaying to and fro and gasping a little, squatting on a bench above a metal cage containing a knot of canvas hockey boots and greying gym shoes. When bed-time came, she thought she ought to stop crying now, she had had her time of release and respite. She must key herself up again. She crept sniffing out into the upper corridors, where Flora Marsh met her and remarked kindly that she looked to be in a bad way. At this Emily gave a great howl, like a wounded creature, and alarmed Flora by staggering from side to side of the corridor as though her sense of balance were gone. Flora could get no sense out of her: Emily was dumb: Flora said perhaps she should go to the nursery, which was what they called the sick bay, should see Sister. After all, they had A-level Latin the next day, she needed her strength. Emily allowed herself to be led through the already-darkened school corridors, moaning a little, thinking, inside her damp and sobbing head in a lucid tic-tac, that she was like an ox, no, like a heifer it would have to be, like Keats's white heifer in the Grecian urn . . . lowing at the skies. . . . Dusty round white lamps hung cheerlessly from metal chains.

Sister was a small, wiry, sensible widow in a white coat and flat rubber-soled shoes. She made Emily a cup of Ovaltine, and put her into an uncomfortable but friendly cane armchair, where Emily went on crying. It became clear to all three of them that there was no prospect of Emily ceasing to cry. The salt tears flooded and filmed her eyes, brimmed over and ran in wet sheets down her face, flowing down her neck in cold streamlets, soaking her collar. The tic-tac in Emily's mind thought of the death of Seneca, the life simply running away, warm and wet, the giving-up. Sister sent Flora Marsh to fetch Emily's things, and Emily, moving her arms like a poor swimmer in thick water, put on her nightdress and climbed into a high hospital bed in the nursery, a hard, cast-iron headed bed, with white cotton blankets. The tears, now silent, darkened and gathered in the pillow. Emily put her knees up to her chin and turned her back on Sister, who pulled back some wet hair, out of her nightdress collar. What has upset her, Sister asked Flora Marsh. Flora didn't know, unless it was something the Headmistress had said. Emily heard them at a huge distance, minute in a waste of waters. Would she be fit to take her exams, Flora asked, and Sister replied, with a night's sleep.

Emily was double. The feeling part had given up, defeated, abandoned to the bliss of dissolution. The thinking part chattered away toughly, tapping out pentameters and alexandrines with and against the soothing flow of the tears. The next morning the feeling part, still watery, accepted tea and toast shakily from Sister; the thinking part looked out craftily from the cavern behind the glistening eyes and stood up, and dressed, and went wet-faced to the Latin exam. There Emily sat, and translated, and scanned, and constructed sentences and paragraphs busily, for a couple of hours. After, a kind of wild hiccup broke in her throat and the tears started again, as though a tap had been turned on, as though something, everything, must be washed away. Emily crept back to the nursery and lay on the iron bed, cold-cheeked and clammy, buffeted by a gale of tags from Horace, storm-cries from *Lear*, domestic inanities from Mrs. Bennett, subjunctives and conditionals, sorting and sifting and arranging them, tic-tac, whilst the tears welled. In this way she wrote two German papers, and the English. She was always ready to write but could never remember what she had written, dissolved in tears, run away. She was like a runner at the end of a marathon, moving on will, not on blood and muscle, who might, if you put out a hand to touch him, fall and not rise again.

She received a visit. There was an empty day between the English and the final French, and Emily lay curled in the iron bed, weeping. Sister had drawn the blinds half-way down the windows, to close out the glare of the summer sun, and the cries of tennis players on the grass courts out in the light. In the room the air was thick and green like clouded glass, with pillars of shadow standing in it, shapes underwater. Miss Crichton-Walker advanced precisely towards the bedside, bringing her own shadow, and the creak of rubber footsteps. Her hair in the half-light glistened green on silver: her dress was mud-coloured, or seemed so, with a little, thickly-crocheted collar. She pulled out a tubular chair and sat down, facing Emily, her hands folded composed in her lap, her knees tightly together, her lips pursed. Crying had not thickened Emily's breathing but vacated its spaces: Miss Crichton-Walker smelled very thinly of mothballs, which, in the context, Emily interpreted as the sharp mustiness of ether or chloroform, a little dizzy. She lay still. Miss Crichton-Walker said, "I am sorry to hear that you are unwell, Emily, if that is the correct term. I am sorry that I was not informed earlier, or I should have come to see you earlier. I should like you to tell me, if you can, why you are so distressed."

"I don't know," said Emily, untruthfully.

"You set high store by these examinations, I know," said the mild voice, accusing. "Perhaps you overreached yourself in some way, overextended yourself, were overambitious. It is a pity, I always think, to force young girls to undergo these arbitrary stresses of judgment when it should surely be possible more accurately to judge the whole tenor of their life and work. Naturally I shall write to the Board of Examiners if you feel—if I feel—you may not quite have done yourself justice. That would be a great disappointment but not a disaster, not by any means a disaster. There is much to be learned in life from temporary setbacks of this kind."

"I have sat all my papers," said Emily's drugged, defensive voice. Miss Crichton-Walker went on.

"I always think that one real failure is necessary to the formation of any really resolved character. You cannot expect to see it that way just now, but I think you will find it so later, if you allow yourself to experience it fully."

Emily knew she must fight, and did not know how. Half of her wanted to respond with a storm of loud crying, to drown this gentle concerned voice with rude noise. Half of her knew, without those words, that that way was disaster, was capitulation, was the acceptance of this last, premature judgment. She said, "If I don't talk, if I just go on, I think I may be all right, I think."

"You do not seem to be all right, Emily."

Emily began to feel faint and dizzy as though the mothballs were indeed anaesthetic. She concentrated on the area

below the judging face: the little knots and gaps in the crochet work, which lay sluggish and inexact, as crochet, even
the best, always will, asymmetrical daisies bordered with
little twisted cords. Little twisted cords of the soft thick
cotton were tied at Miss Crichton-Walker's neck, in a constricting little bow that gathered and flounced the work
and then hung down in two limp strands, each nearly
knotted at its end. Where was Racine, where was the saving thread of reasoned discourse, where the Reader's dry
air? The blinds bellied and swayed slightly. A tapestry of
lines of verse like musical notation ran through Emily's
imagination as though on an endless rolling scroll, the
orderly repetitious screen of the alexandrine somehow
visually mapped by the patterning of Aunt Florrie's exquis-
ite drawn-thread work, little cornsheaves of threads inter-
spersed by cut openings, tied by minute stitches, a lattice, a
trellis.

> *C'était pendant l'horreur d'une profonde nuit.*
> *Ma mère Jézabel devant moi s'est montrée*
> *Comme au jour de sa mort pompeusement parée . . .*

Another bedside vision, highly inappropriate. The thinking Emily smiled in secret, hand under cheek.

"I think I just want to keep quiet, to concentrate . . ."

Miss Crichton-Walker gathered herself, inclining her
silver-green coils slightly towards the recumbent girl.

"I am told that something I said may have upset you. If

that is so, I am naturally very sorry. I do not need to tell you that what I said was well-meant, and, I hope, considered, said in the interest of the majority of the girls, I believe, and not intended to give offence to any. You are all equally my concern, with your varying interests and gifts. It may be that I felt the need of others more at that particular time than your need: perhaps I believed that you were better provided with self-esteem than most. I can assure you that there was no personal application intended. And that I said nothing I do not wholly believe."

"No. Of course not."

"I should like to know whether you did take exception to what I said."

"I don't want to—"

"I don't want to leave you without clearing up this uncomfortable matter. I would hate—I would be very distressed—to think I had caused even unintentional pain to any girl in my charge. Please tell me if you thought I spoke amiss."

"Oh no. No, I didn't. No."

How reluctant a judge, poor Emily, how ill-equipped, how hopeless, to the extent of downright lying, of betraying the principles of exactness. The denial felt like a recantation without there having been an affirmation to recant.

"So now we understand each other. I am very glad. I have brought you some flowers from my little garden: Sister is putting them in water. They should brighten your darkness a little. I hope you will soon feel able to return to the community. I shall keep myself informed of your well-being, naturally."

The French papers were written paragraph by slow paragraph. Emily's pen made dry, black, running little marks on the white paper: Emily's argument threaded itself, a fine line embellished by bright beads of quotations. She did not make it up; she knew it, and recognized it, and laid it out in its ordered pattern. Between paragraphs Emily saw, in the dark corners of the school hall, under dusty shields of honour, little hallucinatory scenes or tableaux, enacting in doorways and window embrasures a charade of the aimlessness of endeavour. She wrote a careful analysis of the clarity of the exposition of Phèdre's devious and confused passion and looked up to see creatures gesticulating on the fringed edge of her consciousness like the blown ghosts trying to pass over the Styx. She saw Miss Crichton-Walker, silvery-muddy, as she had been in the underwater blind-light of the nursery, gravely indicating that failure had its purpose for her. She saw Aunt Florrie, grey and faded and resigned amongst the light thrown off the white linen cloths and immaculate bridal satins of her work, another judge, upright in her chair. She saw Martin, of whom she thought infrequently, on an occasion when he had glee-fully tossed and rumpled all the papers spread on her little table, mild, solid, uncomprehending flesh among falling sheets of white. She saw even the long racks of ghost-glazed, unbaked pots, their pattern hidden beneath the blurred film of watery clay, waiting to go into the furnace of her father's kiln and be cooked into pleasantly clean and shining transparency. Why go on, a soft voice said in her inner ear, what is all this fuss about? What do you know, it asked justly enough, of incestuous maternal passion or the anger of the gods? These are not our concerns: we must make tablecloths and endure. Emily knew about guilt, Miss Crichton-Walker had seen to that, but she did not know about desire, bridled or unbridled, the hooked claws of flame in the blood. She wrote a neat and eloquent paragraph about Phèdre's always-present guilt, arching from the first scene to the end, which led her to feel terror at facing Minos her father, judge of the Underworld, which led her ultimately to feel that the clarity of her vision dirt-ied the light air, the purity of daylight. From time to time, writing this, Emily touched nervously the puffed sacs under her swollen eyes: she was struggling through liquid, she could not help irrelevantly seeing Phèdre's soiled clarity of gaze in terms of her own overwept, sore vision, for which the light was too much.

In another place, the Reader walked in dry, golden air, in his separate desert, waiting to weigh her knowledge and her ignorance, to judge her order and her fallings-off. When Emily had finished her writing she made her bow to him, in her mind, and acknowledged that he was a mythical being, that it was not possible to live in his light.

Who won, you will ask, Emily or Miss Crichton-Walker, since the Reader is mythical and detached, and can neither win nor lose? Emily might be thought to have won, since she had held to her purpose successfully: what she had written was not gibberish but exactly what was required by the scrupulous, checked and counter-checked examiners, so that her marks, when they came, were the highest the school had ever seen. Miss Crichton-Walker might be thought to have won, since Emily was diagnosed as having broken down, was sent home under strict injunctions not to open a book, and was provided by her mother with a piece of petit-point to do through the long summer, a Victorian pattern of blown roses and blue columbine, stretched across a gripping wooden hoop, in which she made dutiful cross after cross blunt-needled, tiny and woollen, pink, buff, crimson, sky-blue, royal blue, Prussian blue, creating on the underside a matted and uncouth weft of lumpy ends and trailing threads, since finishing off neatly was her weakest point. Emily might be thought to have won in the longer run, since she went to university indeed, from where she married young and hastily, having specialized safely in French language. If Emily herself thought that she had somehow lost, she thought this, as is the nature of things, in a fluctuating and intermittent way, feeling also a steady warmth towards her mild husband, a tax inspector, and her two clever daughters, and beyond that a certain limited satisfaction in the translation work she did part-time for various international legal bodies.

One day, however, she was called to see the deputy head of her eldest daughter's school, a shining steel and glass series of cubes and prisms, very different from her own dark, creeper-covered place of education. The deputy head was birdlike, insubstantial and thin in faded denim; his thin grey hair was wispy on his collar; his face was full of mild concern as he explained his anxieties about Emily's daughter. You must try to understand, he told Emily, that just because you are middle-class and university-educated, you need not expect your daughter to share your priorities. I have told Sarah myself that if she wants to be a gardener we shall do everything we can to help her, that her life is her own, that everything all the girls do here is of great importance to us, it all matters equally, all we want is for them to find themselves. Emily said in a small, dull voice that what Sarah wanted was to be able to do advanced French and advanced maths and that she could not really believe that the school had found this impossible to timetable and arrange. The deputy head's expression became extensively gentler and at the same time judicially set. You must allow, he told Emily, that parents are not always the best judge of their child's aptitudes. You may very well—with the best of intentions, naturally—be confusing Sarah's best interests with your own unfulfilled ambitions. Sarah may not be an academic child. Emily dared not ask him, as she should have done, as furious Sarah, frustrated and rebellious, was expecting her to do, if he *knew* Sarah, on what he was founding this judgment. Sarah's French, she said, is very good indeed; it is my subject, I know. She has a natural gift. He smiled his thin disbelief, his professional dismissal, and said that was her view, but not necessarily the school's. We are here to educate the whole human being, he told Emily, to educate her for life, for forming personal relations, running a home, finding her place in society, understanding her responsibilities. We are very much aware of Sarah's needs and problems—one of which, if I may speak frankly, is your expectations. Perhaps you should try to trust us? In any case, it is absolutely impossible to arrange the timetable so that Sarah may do both maths and French.

That old mild voice sounded through this new one: Emily walked away through the glassy-chill corridors thinking that if it had not been for the earlier authority she would have defied this one, wanting to stone the huge, silent panes of glass and let the dry light through, despising her own childishness.

At home, Sarah drew a neat double line under a geometric proof, laid out for the absent scanning of an unfalteringly accurate mind, to whose presence she required access. What Sarah made of herself, what Sarah saw, is Sarah's story. You can believe, I hope, you can afford to believe, that she made her way into its light.

Chapter One
from POSSESSION

These things are there. The garden and the tree
The serpent at its root, the fruit of gold
The woman in the shadow of the boughs
The running water and the grassy space.
They are and were there. At the old world's rim,
In the Hesperidean grove, the fruit
Glowed golden on eternal boughs, and there
The dragon Ladon crisped his jewelled crest
Scraped a gold claw and sharped a silver tooth
And dozed and waited through eternity
Until the tricksy hero, Herakles,
Came to his dispossession and the theft.

—RANDOLPH HENRY ASH
from *The Garden of Proserpina*, 1861

The book was thick and black and covered with dust. Its
boards were bowed and creaking; it had been maltreated in

its own time. Its spine was missing, or, rather, protruded
from amongst the leaves like a bulky marker. It was bandaged about and about with dirty white tape, tied in a neat
bow. The librarian handed it to Roland Michell, who was
sitting waiting for it in the Reading Room of the London
Library. It had been exhumed from Locked Safe no. 5,
where it usually stood between *Pranks of Priapus* and *The
Grecian Way of Love*. It was ten in the morning, one day in
September 1986. Roland had the small single table he liked
best, behind a square pillar, with the clock over the fire-
place nevertheless in full view. To his right was a high sunny
window, through which you could see the high green leaves
of St. James's Square.

The London Library was Roland's favourite place. It was
shabby but civilised, alive with history but inhabited also
by living poets and thinkers who could be found squatting
on the slotted metal floors of the stacks, or arguing pleasantly at the turning of the stair. Here Carlyle had come,
here George Eliot had progressed through the bookshelves.
Roland saw her black silk skirts, her velvet trains, sweeping
compressed between the Fathers of the Church, and heard
her firm foot ring on metal among the German poets.
Here Randolph Henry Ash had come, cramming his elastic
mind and memory with unconsidered trifles from History
and Topography, from the felicitous alphabetical conjunc-
tions of Science and Miscellaneous—Dancing, Deaf and
Dumb, Death, Dentistry, Devil and Demonology, Distribu-
tion, Dogs, Domestic Servants, Dreams. In his day, works

on Evolution had been catalogued under Pre-Adamite
Man. Roland had only recently discovered that the London Library possessed Ash's own copy of Vico's *Principi di
una Scienza Nuova*. Ash's books were most regrettably scat-
tered across Europe and America. By far the largest single
gathering was of course in the Stant Collection at Robert
Dale Owen University in New Mexico, where Mortimer
Cropper worked on his monumental edition of the *Complete Correspondence of Randolph Henry Ash*. That was no
problem nowadays, books travelled the ether like light and
sound. But it was just possible that Ash's own Vico had
marginalia missed even by the indefatigable Cropper. And
Roland was looking for sources for Ash's *Garden of Proserpina*. And there was a pleasure to be had from reading the
sentences Ash had read, touched with his fingers, scanned
with his eyes.

It was immediately clear that the book had been undisturbed for a very long time, perhaps even since it had been
laid to rest. The librarian fetched a checked duster, and
wiped away the dust, a black, thick, tenacious Victorian
dust, a dust composed of smoke and fog particles accumulated before the Clean Air acts. Roland undid the bindings.
The book sprang apart, like a box, disgorging leaf after leaf
of faded paper, blue, cream, grey, covered with rusty writing, the brown scratches of a steel nib. Roland recognised
the handwriting with a shock of excitement. They appeared
to be notes on Vico, written on the backs of book-bills and

letters. The librarian observed that it didn't look as though they had been touched before. Their edges, beyond the pages, were dyed soot-black, giving the impression of the borders of mourning cards. They coincided precisely with their present positions, edge of page and edge of stain.

Roland asked if it was in order for him to study these jottings. He gave his credentials; he was part-time research assistant to Professor Blackadder, who had been editing Ash's *Complete Works* since 1951. The librarian tiptoed away to telephone: whilst he was gone, the dead leaves continued a kind of rustling and shifting, enlivened by their release. Ash had put them there. The librarian came back and said yes, it was quite in order, as long as Roland was very careful not to disturb the sequence of the interleaved fragments until they had been listed and described. The librarian would be glad to know of any important discoveries Mr. Michell might make.

All this was over by ten-thirty. For the next half-hour Roland worked haphazardly, moving backwards and forwards in the Vico, half looking for Proserpina, half reading Ash's notes, which was not easy, since they were written in various languages, in Ash's annotating hand, which was reduced to a minute near-printing, not immediately identifiable as the same as his more generous poetic or letter-writing hand.

At eleven he found what he thought was the relevant passage in Vico. Vico had looked for historical fact in the poetic metaphors of myth and legend; this piecing together was his "new science." His Proserpine was the corn, the origin of commerce and community. Randolph Henry Ash's Proserpine had been seen as a Victorian reflection of religious doubt, a meditation on the myths of resurrection. Lord Leighton had painted her, distraught and floating, a golden figure in a tunnel of darkness. Blackadder had a belief that she represented, for Randolph Ash, a personification of history itself in its early mythical days. (Ash had also written a poem about Gibbon and one about the Venerable Bede, historians of greatly differing kinds. Blackadder had written an article on R. H. Ash and relative historiography.)

Roland compared Ash's text with the translation, and copied parts onto an index card. He had two boxes of these, tomato-red and an intense grassy green, with springy plastic hinges that popped in the library silence.

Ears of grain were called apples of gold, which must have been the first gold in the world while metallic gold was unknown. . . . So the golden apple which Hercules first brought back or gathered from Hesperia must have been grain; and the Gallic Hercules with links of this gold, that issue from his mouth, chains men by the ears: something which will later be discovered as a myth concerning the fields. Hence Hercules remained the Deity to propitiate in order to find treasures, whose god was Dis (identical with

Pluto) who carries off Proserpine (another name for Ceres or grain) to the underworld described by the poets, according to whom its first name was Styx, its second the land of the dead, its third the depth of furrows. . . . It was of this golden apple that Virgil, most learned in heroic antiquities, made the golden bough Aeneas carries into the Inferno or Underworld.

Randolph Henry Ash's Proserpina, "gold-skinned in the gloom," was also "grain-golden." Also "bound with golden links" which might have been jewellery or chains. Roland wrote neat cross-references under the headings of grain, apples, chain, treasure. Folded into the page of Vico on which the passage appeared was a bill for candles on the back of which Ash had written: "The individual appears for an instant, joins the community of thought, modifies it and dies; but the species, that dies not, reaps the fruit of his ephemeral existence." Roland copied this out and made another card, on which he interrogated himself: "*Query*? Is this a quotation or is it Ash himself? Is Proserpina the Species? A very C19 idea. Or is she the individual? When did he put these papers in here? Are they pre- or post-*The Origin of Species*? Not conclusive anyway—he cd have been interested in Development generally. . . ."

That was eleven-fifteen. The clock ticked, motes of dust danced in sunlight, Roland meditated on the tiresome and bewitching endlessness of the quest for knowledge. Here

he sat, recuperating a dead man's reading, timing his explo-
ration by the library clock and the faint constriction of his
belly. (Coffee is not to be had in the London Library.) He
would have to show all this new treasure-trove to Blackadder, who would be both elated and grumpy, who would
anyway be pleased that it was locked away in Safe 5 and not
spirited away to Robert Dale Owen University in Harmony City, with so much else. He was reluctant to tell
Blackadder. He enjoyed possessing his knowledge on his
own. Proserpina was between pages 288 and 289. Under
page 300 lay two folded complete sheets of writing paper.
Roland opened these delicately. They were both letters in
Ash's flowing hand, both headed with his Great Russell
Street address and dated, June 21st. No year. Both began
"Dear Madam," and both were unsigned. One was considerably shorter than the other.

Dear Madam,

*Since our extraordinary conversation I have thought of nothing
else. It has not often been given to me as a poet, it is perhaps not
often given to human beings, to find such ready sympathy, such
wit and judgment together. I write with a strong sense of the neces-
sity of continuing our talk, and without premeditation, under the
impression that you were indeed as much struck as I was by our
quite extraordinary to ask if it would be possible for me to call on
you, perhaps one day next week. I feel, I know with a certainty
that cannot be the result of folly or misapprehension, that you and*

I must speak again. I know you go out in company very little, and was the more fortunate that dear Crabb managed to entice you to his breakfast table. To think that amongst the babble of undergraduate humour and through all Crabb's well-wrought anecdotes, even including the Bust, we were able to say so much, that was significant, simply to each other. I cannot surely be alone in feeling

The second one ran:

Dear Madam,

Since our pleasant and unexpected conversation I have thought of little else. Is there any way in which it can be resumed, more privately and at more leisure? I know you go out in company very little, and was the more fortunate that dear Crabb managed to entice you to his breakfast table. How much I owe to his continuing good health, that he should feel able and eager, at eighty-two years of age, to entertain poets and undergraduates and mathematical professors and political thinkers so early in the day, and to tell the anecdote of the Bust with his habitual fervour without too much delaying the advent of buttered toast.

Did you not find it as strange as I did, that we should so immediately understand each other so well? For we did understand each other uncommonly well, did we not? Or is this perhaps a product of the over-excited brain of a middle-aged and somewhat disparaged poet, when he finds that his ignored, his arcane, his deviously perspicuous meanings, which he thought not meanings, since no one appeared able to understand them, had after all one clear-eyed and amused reader and judge? What you said of Alexander Selkirk's monologue, the good sense you made of the ramblings of my John Bunyan, your understanding of the passion of Iñez de Castro . . . gruesomely resurrecta . . . but that is enough of my egoistical mutter, and of those of my personae, who are not, as you so rightly remarked, my masks. I would not have you think that I do not recognise the superiority of your own fine ear and finer taste. I am convinced that you must undertake that grand Fairy Topic—you will make something highly strange and original of it. In connection with that, I wonder if you have thought of Vico's history of the primitive races—of his idea that the ancient gods and later heroes are personifications of the fates and aspirations of the people rising in figures from the common mind? Something here might be made of your Fairy's legendary rootedness in veritable castles and genuine agricultural reform— one of the queerest aspects of her story, to a modern mind. But I run on again; assuredly you have determined on your own best ways of presenting the topic, you who are so wise and learned in your retirement.

I cannot but feel, though it may be an illusion induced by the delectable drug of understanding, ~~that you must in some way share my eagerness that further conversation could be mutually profitable that we must meet. I cannot~~ do not think I ~~am~~ can be mistaken in my belief that our meeting was also ~~important~~ interesting to you, and that however much you may value your seclusion

I know that you came only to honour dear Crabb, at a small informal party, because he had been of assistance to your illustrious Father, and valued his work at a time when it meant a great

deal to him. But you did come out, so I may hope that you can
be induced to vary your quiet with
   I am sure you understand

Roland was first profoundly shocked by these writings, and then, in his scholarly capacity, thrilled. His mind busied itself automatically with dating and placing this unachieved dialogue with an unidentified woman. There was no year on the letters, but they must necessarily come after the publication of Ash's dramatic poems, *Gods, Men and Heroes*, which had appeared in 1856 and had not, contrary to Ash's hopes and perhaps expectations, found favour with the reviewers, who had declared his verses obscure, his tastes perverse and his people extravagant and improbable. "The Solitary Thoughts of Alexander Selkirk" was one of those poems, the musings of the castaway sailor on his island. So was "The Tinker's Grace," purporting to be Bunyan's prison musings on Divine Grace, and so was Pedro of Portugal's rapt and bizarre declaration of love, in 1356, for the embalmed corpse of his murdered wife, Iñez de Castro, who swayed beside him on his travels, leather-brown and skeletal, crowned with lace and gold circlet, hung about with chains of diamonds and pearls, her bone-fingers fantastically ringed. Ash liked his characters at or over the edge of madness, constructing systems of belief and survival from the fragments of experience available to them. It would be possible, Roland thought, to identify the breakfast party, which must have been one of Crabb Robinson's later efforts to provide stimulating conversation for the students of the new London University.

Crabb Robinson's papers were kept in Dr. Williams's Library in Gordon Square, originally designed as University Hall, supported by Robinson as a place in which lay students could experience collegiate university life. It would, it must, be easy to check in Robinson's diary an occasion on which Ash had breakfasted at 30 Russell Square with a professor of mathematics, a political thinker (Bagehot?) and a reclusive lady who knew about, who wrote, or proposed to write, poetry.

He had no idea who she might be. Christina Rossetti? He thought not. He was not sure that Miss Rossetti would have approved of Ash's theology, or of his sexual psychology. He could not identify the Fairy Topic, either, and this gave him a not uncommon sensation of his own huge ignorance, a grey mist, in which floated or could be discerned odd glimpses of solid objects, odd bits of glitter of domes or shadows of roofs in the gloom.

Had the correspondence continued? If it had, where was it, what jewels of information about Ash's "ignored, arcane, deviously perspicuous meanings" might not be revealed by it? Scholarship might have to reassess all sorts of certainties. On the other hand, had the correspondence ever in fact started? Or had Ash finally floundered in his inability to express his sense of urgency? It was this urgency above all that moved and shocked Roland. He thought he knew Ash fairly well, as well as anyone might know a man whose life seemed to be all in his mind, who lived a quiet and exemplary married life for forty years, whose correspondence was voluminous indeed, but guarded, courteous and not of the most lively. Roland liked that in Randolph Henry Ash. He was excited by the ferocious vitality and darting breadth of reference of the work, and secretly, personally, he was rather pleased that all this had been achieved out of so peaceable, so unruffled a private existence.

He read the letters again. Had a final draft been posted? Or had the impulse died or been rebuffed? Roland was seized by a strange and uncharacteristic impulse of his own. It was suddenly quite impossible to put these living words back into page 300 of Vico and return them to Safe 5. He looked about him: no one was looking: he slipped the letters between the leaves of his own copy of the Oxford Selected Ash, which he was never without. Then he returned to the Vico annotations, transferring the most interesting methodically to his card index, until the clanging bell descended the stairwell, signifying the end of the study. He had forgotten about his lunch.

When he left, with his green and tomato boxes heaped on his Selected Ash, they nodded affably from behind the issue desk. They were used to him. There were notices about mutilation of volumes, about theft, with which he quite failed to associate himself. He left the building as usual, his battered and bulging briefcase under his arm. He climbed on a 14 bus in Piccadilly, and went upstairs, clutching his booty. Between Piccadilly and Putney, where he lived in the basement of a decaying Victorian house, he progressed through his usual states of somnolence, sick juddering wakefulness, and increasing worry about Val.

Chapter Two
from POSSESSION

A man is the history of his breaths and thoughts, acts, atoms and wounds, love, indifference and dislike; also of his race and nation, the soil that fed him and his forebears, the stones and sands of his familiar places, long-silenced battles and struggles of conscience, of the smiles of girls and the slow utterance of old women, of accidents and the gradual action of inexorable law, of all this and something else too, a single flame which in every way obeys the laws that pertain to Fire itself, and yet is lit and put out from one moment to the next, and can never be relumed in the whole waste of time to come.

So Randolph Henry Ash, *ca* 1840, when he was writing *Ragnarök*, a poem in twelve books, which some saw as a Christianising of the Norse myth and some trounced as atheistic and diabolically despairing. It mattered to Randolph Ash what a man was, though he could, without

undue disturbance, have written that general pantechnicon of a sentence using other terms, phrases and rhythms
and have come in the end to the same satisfactory evasive
metaphor. Or so Roland thought, trained in the post-
structuralist deconstruction of the subject. If he had been
asked what Roland Michell was, he would have had to
give a very different answer.

In 1986 he was twenty-nine, a graduate of Prince Albert
College, London (1978) and a PhD of the same university
(1985). His doctoral dissertation was entitled *History, Historians and Poetry? A Study of the Presentation of Historical "Evidence" in the Poems of Randolph Henry Ash*. He had written it
under the supervision of James Blackadder, which had
been a discouraging experience. Blackadder was discouraged and liked to discourage others. (He was also a strin-
gent scholar.) Roland was now employed, part-time, in
what was known as Blackadder's Ash Factory (why not
Ashram? Val had said), which operated from the British
Museum, to which Ash's wife, Ellen, had given many of
the manuscripts of his poems, when he died. The Ash Factory was funded by a small grant from London University
and a much larger one from the Newsome Foundation in
Albuquerque, a charitable trust of which Mortimer Cropper was a trustee. This might appear to indicate that Blackadder and Cropper worked harmoniously together on behalf
of Ash. This would be a misconception. Blackadder believed
Cropper to have designs on those manuscripts lodged
with, but not owned by, the British Library, and to be

worming his way into the confidence and goodwill of the owners by displays of munificence and helpfulness. Blackadder, a Scot, believed British writings should stay in Britain and be studied by the British. It may seem odd to begin a description of Roland Michell with an excursus into the complicated relations of Blackadder, Cropper and Ash, but it was in these terms that Roland most frequently thought of himself. When he did not think in terms of Val.

He thought of himself as a latecomer. He had arrived too late for things that were still in the air but vanished, the whole ferment and brightness and journeyings and youth of the 1960s, the blissful dawn of what he and his contemporaries saw as a pretty blank day. Through the psychedelic years he was a schoolboy in a depressed Lancashire cotton town, untouched alike by Liverpool noise and London turmoil. His father was a minor official in the County Council. His mother was a disappointed English graduate. He thought of himself as though he were an application form, for a job, a degree, a life, but when he thought of his mother, the adjective would not be expurgated. She was disappointed. In herself, in his father, in him. The wrath of her disappointment had been the instrument of his education, which had taken place in a perpetual rush from site to site of a hastily amalgamated three-school comprehensive, the Aneurin Bevan school, combining Glasdale Old Grammar School, St Thomas à Becket's C of E Secondary School and the Clothiers' Guild Technical Modern School. His mother had drunk too much stout, "gone up the school,"

and had him transferred from metal work to Latin, from
Civic Studies to French; she had paid a maths coach with
the earnings of a paper-round she had sent him out on.
And so he had acquired an old-fashioned classical education, with gaps where teachers had been made redundant
or classroom chaos had reigned. He had done what was
hoped of him, always, had four A's at A Level, a First, a
PhD. He was now essentially unemployed, scraping a living
on part-time tutoring, dogsbodying for Blackadder and
some restaurant dishwashing. In the expansive 1960s he
would have advanced rapidly and involuntarily, but now he
saw himself as a failure and felt vaguely responsible for this.
He was a compact, clearcut man, with precise features, a
lot of very soft black hair, and thoughtful dark brown eyes.
He had a look of wariness, which could change when he
felt relaxed or happy, which was not often in these difficult
days, into a smile of amused friendliness and pleasure which
aroused feelings of warmth, and something more, in many
women. He was generally unaware of these feelings, since
he paid little attention to what people thought about him,
which was part of his attraction. Val called him Mole,
which he disliked. He had never told her so.

He lived with Val, whom he had met at a Freshers' tea
party in the Student Union when he was eighteen. He
believed now, though this belief may have been a mythic
smoothing of his memory, that Val was the first person his
undergraduate self had spoken to, socially that was, not

officially. He had liked the look of her, he remembered, a soft, brown uncertain look. She had been standing on her own, holding a teacup in front of her, not looking about her, but rather fixedly out of the window, as though she expected no one to approach and invited no one. She projected a sort of calm, a lack of strife, and so he went over to join her. And since then they had never not been together. They signed up for the same courses and joined the same societies; they sat together in seminars and went together to the National Film Theatre; they had sex together and moved together into a one-roomed flat in their second year. They lived frugally off a diet of porridge and lentils and beans and yogurt; they drank a little beer, making it spin out; they shared book-buying; they were both entirely confined to their grants, which did not go far in London, and could not be supplemented with holiday earnings, for these had vanished with the oil crisis. Val had been, Roland was sure, partly responsible for his First. (Along with his mother and Randolph Henry Ash.) She simply expected it of him, she made him always say what he thought, she argued points, she worried constantly about whether she was, whether they both were, working hard enough. They quarreled hardly at all and when they did it was almost always because Roland expressed concern about Val's reserve with the world in general, her refusal to advance opinions in class and, later, even to him. In the early days she had had lots of quiet opinions, he remem-

bered, which she had offered him, shyly slyly, couched as a
kind of invitation or bait. There had been poems she had
liked. Once she had sat up naked in his dark digs and
recited Robert Graves:

> *She tells her love while half asleep,*
> *In the dark hours,*
> *With half-words whispered low:*
> *As Earth stirs in her winter sleep*
> *And puts out grass and flowers*
> *Despite the snow,*
> *Despite the falling snow.*

She had a rough voice gentled, between London and Liverpool, as the group voice was. When Roland began to
speak, after this, she put a hand over his mouth, which was
as well, for he had nothing to say. Later, Roland noticed, as
he himself had his successes, Val said less and less, and when
she argued, offered him increasingly his own ideas, sometimes the reverse side of the knitting, but essentially his.
She even wrote her Required Essay on "Male Ventriloquism: The Women of Randolph Henry Ash." Roland
did not want this. When he suggested that she should strike
out on her own, make herself noticed, speak up, she accused
him of "taunting" her. When he asked, what did she mean,
"taunting," she resorted, as she always did when they argued,
to silence. Since silence was also Roland's only form of
aggression, they would continue in this way for days, or,

one terrible time when Roland directly criticized "Male Ventriloquism," for weeks. And then the fraught silence would modulate into conciliatory monosyllable, and back to their peaceful co-existence. When Finals came, Roland did steadily and predictably well. Val's papers were bland and minimal, in large confident handwriting, well laid out. "Male Ventriloquism" was judged to be good work and discounted by the examiners as probably largely by Roland, which was doubly unjust, since he had refused to look at it, and did not agree with its central proposition, which was that Randolph Henry Ash neither liked nor understood women, that his female speakers were constructs of his own fear and aggression, that even the poem-cycle, *Ask to Embla*, was the work not of love but of narcissism, the poet addressing his Anima. (No biographical critic had ever satisfactorily identified Embla.) Val did very badly. Roland had supposed she had expected this, but it became dreadfully obvious that she had not. There were tears, night-long, choked, whimpering tears, and the first tantrum.

Val left him for the first time since they set up house, and went briefly "home." Home was Croydon, where she lived with her divorced mother in a council flat, supported by social security, supplemented occasionally by haphazard maintenance payments from her father, who was in the Merchant Navy and had not been seen since Val was five. Val had never, during their time together, proposed to Roland that they visit her mother, though Roland had twice taken her to Glasdale, where she had helped his

father wash up, and had taken his mother's jeering defla-
tion of their way of life in her stride, telling him, "Don't
worry, Mole. I've seen it all before. Only mine drinks. If
you lit a match in our kitchen, it'd go up with a roar."

When Val was gone, Roland realised, with a shock like a
religious conversion, that he did not want their way of life
to go on. He rolled over, and spread his loosened limbs in
the bed, he opened windows, he went to the Tate Gallery
alone and looked at the dissolving blue and gold air of
Turner's Norham Castle. He cooked a pheasant for his rival
in the departmental rat-race, Fergus Wolff, which was
exciting and civilised, although the pheasant was tough
and full of shot. He made plans, which were not plans,
but visions of solitary activity and free watchfulness, things
he had never had. After a week, Val came back, tearful and
shaky, and declared that she meant at least to earn her living, and would take a course in shorthand-typing. "At least
you want me," she told Roland, her face damp and glistening. "I don't know why you should want me, I'm no
good, but you do." "Of course I do," Roland had said.
"Of course."

When his DES grant ran out, Val became the breadwinner,
whilst he finished his PhD. She acquired an IBM golfball
typewriter and did academic typing at home in the
evenings and various well-paid temping jobs during the
day. She worked in the City and in teaching hospitals, in

shipping firms and art galleries. She resisted pressure to specialize. She would not be drawn out to talk about her work, to which she almost never referred without the adjective "menial." "I must do just a few more menial things before I go to bed" or, more oddly, "I was nearly run over on my menial way this morning." Her voice acquired a jeering note, not unfamiliar to Roland, who wondered for the first time what his mother had been like *before* her disappointment, which in her case was his father and to some extent himself. The typewriter clashed and harried him at night, never rhythmical enough to be ignored.

There were now two Vals. One sat silently at home in old jeans and unevenly hanging long crêpey shirts, splashed with murky black and purple flowers. This one had lustre-less brown hair, very straight, hanging about a pale, underground face. Just sometimes, this one had crimson nails, left over from the other, who wore a tight black skirt and a black jacket with padded shoulders over a pink silk shirt and was carefully made up with pink and brown eyeshadow, brushed blusher along the cheekbone and plummy lips. This mournfully bright menial Val wore high heels and a black beret. She had beautiful ankles, invisible under the domestic jeans. Her hair was rolled into a passable page-boy and sometimes tied with a black ribbon. She stopped short of perfume. She was not constructed to be attractive. Roland half wished that she was, that a merchant banker would take her out to dinner, or a shady solicitor to the Playboy Club. He hated himself for these demeaning fantasies, and was reasonably afraid that she might suspect he nourished them.

If he could get a job, it might be easier to initiate some change. He made applications and was regularly turned down. When one came up in his own department there were six hundred applications. Roland was interviewed, out of courtesy he decided, but the job went to Fergus Wolff, whose track record was less consistent, who could be brilliant or bathetic, but never dull and right, who was loved by his teachers, whom he exasperated and entranced, where Roland excited no emotion more passionate than solid approbation. Fergus was also in the right field, which was literary theory. Val was more indignant than Roland about this event, and her indignation upset him as much as his own failure, for he liked Fergus and wanted to be able to go on liking him. Val found one of her insisting words for Fergus too, one which was askew and inaccurate. "That pretentious blond bombshell" she said of him. "That pretentious sexpot." She liked to use sexist wolf-whistle words as a kind of boomerang. This embarrassed Roland, since Fergus transcended any such terminology; he was indeed blond, and he was indeed sexually very successful, and that was an end to it. He came to no more meals, and Roland feared Fergus thought this was a function of his, Roland's, resentment.

When he got home that evening he could smell that Val was in a mood. The basement was full of the sharp warmth of frying onions, which meant she was cooking something complicated. When she was not in a mood, when she was apathetic, she opened tins or boiled eggs, or at most dressed an avocado. When she was either very cheerful or very angry, she cooked. She stood at the sink, chopping courgettes and aubergines, when he came in, and did not look up, so he surmised that the mood was bad. He put down his bag quietly. They had a cavernous basement room, which they had painted apricot and white to cheer it up; it was furnished with a double divan, two very old armchairs with curvaceous rolled arms and head-rests, plum and plushy and dusty, a second-hand stained-oak office desk, where Roland worked, and a newer varnished beech desk, where the typewriter sat. These were back to back on the long side-walls each with their Habitat anglepoise, Roland's black, Val's rose-pink. On the back wall were bookcases, made of bricks and planks, sagging under standard texts, most of them jointly owned, some duplicated. They had put up various posters: a British Museum poster from the *Koran*, intricate and geometric, a Tate advertisement for a Turner exhibition.

Roland possessed three images of Randolph Henry Ash. One, a photograph of the death mask, which was one of the central pieces in the Stant Collection of Harmony City, stood on his desk. There was a puzzle about how this bleak, broad-browed carved head had come into existence, since there also existed a photograph of the poet in his last sleep, still patriarchally bearded. Who had shaved him,

when? Roland had wondered, and Mortimer Cropper had
asked in his biography, *The Great Ventriloquist*, without finding an answer. His other two portraits were photographic
copies, made to order, of the two portraits of Ash in the
National Portrait Gallery. Val had banished these to the
dark of the hall. She said she did not want him staring at
her, she wanted a bit of her life to herself, without having
to share it with Randolph Ash.

In the dark hall the pictures were difficult to see. One
was by Manet and one was by G. F. Watts. The Manet had
been painted when the painter was in England in 1867,
and had some things in common with his portrait of Zola.
He had shown Ash, whom he had met previously in Paris,
sitting at his desk, in a three-quarters profile, in a carved
mahogany chair. Behind him was a kind of triptych with
ferny foliage, to the left and right, enclosing a watery space
in which rosy and silver fish shone between pondweeds.
The effect was partly to set the poet amongst the roots
of a wood or forest, until, as Mortimer Cropper had
pointed out, one realised that the background was one of
those compartmentalised Wardian cases, in which the Vic-
torians grew plants in controlled environments, or created
self-sustaining ponds, in order to study the physiology of
plants and fishes. Manet's Ash was dark, powerful, with
deepset eyes under a strong brow, a vigorous beard and a
look of confident private amusement. He looked watchful
and intelligent, not ready to move in a hurry. In front of
him on his desk were disposed various objects, an elegant

and masterly still life to complement the strong head and the ambivalent natural growths. There was a heap of rough geological specimens, including two almost spherical stones, a little like cannon balls, one black and one a sulphurous yellow, some ammonites and trilobites, a large crystal ball, a green glass inkwell, the articulated skeleton of a cat, a heap of books, two of which could be seen to be the *Divina Commedia* and *Faust*, and an hourglass in a wooden frame. Of these, the inkwell, the crystal ball, the hourglass, the two named books and two of the others, which had been painstakingly identified as *Quixote* and Lyell's *Geology*, were now in the Stant Collection, where a room had been arranged, Wardian cases and all, to resemble the Manet setting. The chair had also been collected, and the desk itself.

The portrait by Watts was mistier and less authoritative. It had been painted in 1876 and showed an older and more ethereal poet, his head rising, as is common with Watts's portraits, from a vague dark column of a body into a spiritual light. There was a background but it had darkened. In the original portrait it could be vaguely made out as a kind of craggy wild place; in this photographic reproduction it was no more than thickenings and glimmerings in the black. The important features of this image were the eyes, which were large and gleaming, and the beard, a riverful of silvers and creams, whites and blue-greys, channels and forks resembling da Vinci's turbulences, the apparent source of light. Even in the photograph, it shone. Roland considered Randolph Ash, who had always looked so self-possessed, so all-of-a-piece. The look of amusement Manet had captured now took on an almost teasing aspect, a challenge: "So you think you know me?" And the urgency of the unfinished letters gave a new energy to the solid dark body, as though it might after all be capable of violent movement. The known Ash shifted a little, and Roland felt flickers of excitement of his own. A kind of readiness. A kind of fear.

At the end of the room the window opened onto a little yard, with steps to the garden, which was visible between railings in the upper third of their window. Their flat was described as a garden flat when they came to see it, which was the only occasion on which they were asked to come into the garden, into which they were later told they had no right to entry. They were not even allowed to attempt to grow things in tubs in their back area, for reasons vague but peremptory, put forward by their landlady, an octogenarian Mrs. Irving, who inhabited the three floors above them in a rank civet fug amongst unnumbered cats, and who kept the garden as bright and wholesome and well ordered as her living-room was sparse and decomposing. She had enticed them in like an old witch, Val said, by talking volubly to them in the garden about the quietness of the place, giving them each a small, gold, furry apricot from the espaliered trees along the curving brick wall. The garden was long, thin, bowery, with sunny spots of grass, surrounded by little box hedges, its air full of roses, swarthy damask, thick ivory, floating pink, its borders restraining fantastic striped and spotted lilies, curling bronze and gold, bold and hot and rich. And forbidden. But they did not know that in the beginning, as Mrs. Irving expatiated in her cracked and gracious voice on the high brick wall which dated from the Civil War, when it had formed one boundary of General Fairfax's lands. Randolph Henry Ash had written a poem purporting to be spoken by a Digger in Putney. He had even come there to look at the river at low tide, it was in Ellen Ash's Journal, they had brought a picnic of chicken and parsley pie. That fact, and the conjunction of Marvell's patron, Fairfax, with the existence of the walled garden of fruit and flowers were enough to tempt Roland and Val into the garden flat, with its prohibited view.

In spring their window was lit from above by the yellow glow of a thick row of bright daffodils. Tendrils of Virginia creeper crept down as far as the window-frame, and progressed on little circular suckers across the glass, at huge vegetable speed. Swathes of jasmine, loose from a prolifically flowering specimen on the edge of the house, occasionally fell over their railing, with their sweet scent, before Mrs. Irving, clothed in her gardening gear of wellingtons and apron over the seated and threadbare tweed suit in which she had first enticed them in, came and bound these back. Roland had once asked her if he could help in the garden, in exchange for the right to sit there sometimes. He had been told that he didn't know the first thing about it, that the young were all the same, destructive and careless, that Mrs. Irving set a value on her privacy. "You would think," said Val, "that the cats would do the garden no good." That was before they found the patches of damp on their own kitchen and bathroom ceilings, which, when touched with a finger, smelled unmistakably of cat-piss. The cats too, were under prohibition, confined to quarters. Roland thought they ought to look for somewhere else, but held back from proposing it, because he was not the breadwinner, and because he didn't want to do anything so decisive, in terms of himself and Val.

Val put before him grilled marinated lamb, ratatouille and hot Greek bread. He said, "Shall I get a bottle of wine?" and Val said, disagreeably and truthfully, "You should have thought of that some time back; it'll all go cold." They ate at a card-table, which they unfolded and folded again, after.

"I made an amazing discovery today," he told her.

"Oh?"

"I was in the London Library. They've got R. H. Ash's Vico. His own copy. They keep it in the safe. I had it brought up and it was absolutely bursting at the seams with his own notes, all tucked in, on the backs of bills and things. And I'm ninety per cent sure no one had looked at them, ever, not since he put them there, because all the edges were black and the lines coincided. . . ."

"How interesting." Flatly.

"It might change the face of scholarship. It *could*. They let me read them, they didn't take it away. I'm sure no one knew it was all there."

"I expect they didn't."

"I'll have to tell Blackadder. He'll want to see how important it is, make sure Cropper hasn't been there. . . ."

"I expect he will, yes."

It was a bad mood.

"I'm sorry, Val, I'm sorry to bore you. It does look exciting."

"That depends what turns you on. We all have our little pleasures of different kinds, I suppose."

"I can write it up. An article. A solid discovery. Make me a better job prospect."

"There aren't any jobs." She added, "And if there are, they go to Fergus Wolff."

He knew his Val: he had watched her honourably try to prevent herself from adding that last remark.

"If you really think what I do is so unimportant. . . ."

"You do what turns you on," said Val. "Everyone does, if they're lucky, if there is anything that turns them on. You have this thing about this dead man. Who had a thing about dead people. That's OK but not everyone is very bothered about all that. I see some things, from my menial vantage point. Last week, when I was in that ceramics export place, I found some photographs under a file in my boss's desk. Things being done to little boys. With chains and gags and—dirt— This week, ever so efficiently filing records for this surgeon, I just happened to come across a sixteen-year-old who had his leg off last year—they're fitting him with an artificial one, it takes months, they're incredibly slow—and it's started up for certain now in his other leg, he doesn't know, but I know, I know lots of things. None of them fit together, none of them makes any sense. There was a man who went off to Amsterdam to buy some diamonds, I helped his secretary book his ticket, first class, and his limousine, smooth as clockwork, and as he's walking along a canal admiring the housefronts someone stabs him in the back, destroys a kidney, gangrene sets in, now he's dead. Just like that. Chaps like those use my menial services, here today, gone tomorrow. Randolph Ash wrote long ago. Forgive me if I don't care what he wrote in his Vico."

"Oh, Val, such horrible things, you never say—"

"Oh, it's all very *interesting*, my menial keyhole observations, make no mistake. Just it doesn't make sense and it leaves me nowhere. I suppose I envy you, piecing together old Ash's world-picture. Only where does that leave *you*, old Mole? What's *your* world-picture? And how are you ever going to afford to get us away from dripping cat-piss and being *on top of each other?*"

Something had upset her, Roland reasonably deduced. Something that had caused her to use the phrase "turn you

on" several times, which was uncharacteristic. Perhaps someone had grabbed her. Or had not done so. No, that was
unworthy. Anger and petulance *did* turn her on, he knew.
He knew more than was quite good for him about Val. He
went across and stroked the nape of her neck, and she
sniffed and stiffened and then relaxed. After a bit, they
moved over to the bed.

He had not told her, and could not tell her, about his secret
theft. Late that night, he looked at the letters again, in the
bathroom. "Dear Madam, Since our extraordinary conversation I have thought of nothing else." "Dear Madam,
Since our pleasant and unexpected conversation I have
thought of little else." Urgent, unfinished. Shocking. Roland
had never been much interested in Randolph Henry Ash's
vanished body; he did not spend time visiting his house in
Russell Street, or sitting where he had sat, on stone garden
seats; that was Cropper's style. What Roland liked was his
knowledge of the movements of Ash's mind, stalked through
the twists and turns of his syntax, suddenly sharp and clear
in an unexpected epithet. But these dead letters troubled
him, physically even, because they were only beginnings.
He did not imagine Randolph Henry Ash, his pen moving
rapidly across the paper, but he did have the thought of the
pads of the long-dead fingers that had held and folded these
half-covered sheets, before preserving them in the book,
instead of jettisoning them. *Who?* He must try to find out.

GEORGE ELIOT:
A CELEBRATION

My first introduction to George Eliot was unpropitious. At the age of eleven I underwent a class "reading" of *Silas Marner* at Sheffield High School and remember finding it very tedious: no drama, or what there might have been subdued, too many comic country people who bore little relation to anyone I, a city child, had met, no romance of the simple sort I was looking for. In bed I read Scott, Jane Austen, Dickens, endless historical romances and a lot of poems. I was quite incapable of appreciating the economy and sober order of *Silas*. I don't think, although it's a legendary Tale, it should be given to children. Then I read *The Mill on the Floss*, which I found unbearable for different reasons. I didn't like the beginning because of its inexorable damping-down of the fire and energy of a lonely, clever girl. I didn't like the end, because it didn't seem appropriate: drowning *with her brother* was not (and I must say, is not) a fate for Maggie Tulliver that leaves one with any feeling of having really come to the end—tragic, passionate, despondent—of the complexities of cross, clever, ferocious Maggie. The author drowned the heroine for dramatic reasons—and I, as a child reader, felt cheated. So I didn't persevere.

When I was at Cambridge, good undergraduates were learning about the Great Tradition of the English novel from F. R. Leavis. Jane Austen, George Eliot, D. H. Lawrence, Henry James, Conrad. *Not*, in those days, Dickens or Scott, my early loves, and only one Brontë—Emily. I played safe by avoiding the whole issue and worked with poetry almost exclusively. So I came to George Eliot late, in the days when I was teaching the modern English novel in evening classes and trying to find out how to write a good novel myself. Meeting any great author is like being made aware of freedoms and capabilities one had no idea were possible. Reading *Middlemarch* and *Daniel Deronda* I learned several primitive yet crucial lessons about writing novels— and these lessons were also moral lessons about life. It is possible, I learned, to invent a world peopled by *a large number* of interrelated people, almost all of whose processes of thought, developments of consciousness, biological anxieties, sense of their past and future can most scrupulously be made available to readers, can work with and against each other, can lead to failure, or partial failure, or triumphant growth.

I suppose I was in my late twenties when I began teaching *Middlemarch*, and I taught it with passion because I perceived it was about the growth, use and inevitable failure and frustration of all human energy—a lesson one is not interested in at eleven or eighteen, but at twenty-six, with two small children, it seems crucial. George Eliot's people were appallingly ambitious and greedy—not always for political or even, exclusively, sexual power, as in most of the other English novels I read. They were ambitious to use their minds to the full, to discover something, to live on a scale where their life felt valuable from moment to moment. In *Middlemarch* Dorothea, the untutored woman who wishes to contribute to science, even Casaubon, the failed scholar, had hopes which meant something to *me*, as Madame Bovary's cramped, Romantic, confused sexual lunges towards more life did not. In *Daniel Deronda* the hero has humane and intellectual ambitions: Gwendolen Harleth is a sympathetic portrait on the grand scale of a deficient being whose conceptions of the use of energy never extended beyond power (sexual and social) and money (not for its own sake, but for social pride). Perhaps the most vital discovery I made about George Eliot at that time was that her people *think*: they worry an idea, they are, within their limits, responsive to politics and art and philosophy and history.

The next discovery was that the author thought. One of the technical things I had discovered during the early teaching of *Middlemarch* was George Eliot's authorial interventions, which were then very unfashionable, thought to be pompous Victorian moralizing and nasty lumps in the flow of "the story." I worked out that on the contrary, the authorial "voice" added all sorts of freedom a good writer could do with. Sometimes it could work with firm irony to undercut the sympathetic "inner" portrayal of a character. Consider this early description of Dorothea:

> Her mind was theoretic, and yearned by its nature after some lofty conception of the world which might frankly include the parish of Tipton and her own rule of conduct there; she was enamoured of intensity and greatness, and rash in embracing whatever seemed to her to have those aspects; likely to seek martyrdom, to make retractions, and then to incur martyrdom after all in a quarter where she had not sought it. Certainly such elements in the character of a marriageable girl tended to interfere with her lot, and hinder it from being decided according to custom, by good looks, vanity, and merely canine affection.

There is so much in there, in the style. The magisterial authority of a Greek Chorus, or God, who knows Dorothea's fate before her drama has really begun. Sympathy, in the author, towards the character's ambitions, and a certain wry sense that, unfocused as they are, they are doomed. And then, in that last sentence, which is biting social comedy, the choice of the crucial adjective—"merely *canine* affection"—to disparage the kind of "love" thought adequate by most planners or marriages, not only in the nineteenth century.

From close study of the novels, I went on to the life and read George Eliot's essays, written for the large part for the liberal *Westminster Review* in the years immediately preceding her shocking elopement with the married G. H. Lewes. They are intellectual, yes, and learned—very learned. George Eliot read Latin, Greek, French, Spanish, Italian and German: she was *au fait* with current philosophy, physiology, psychology and sociology: she wrote with ferocious authority. I liked that—I admire the deployment of a clear mind and a lot of information as one might admire Rembrandt's mastery of colour, chiaroscuro, space. But what is also marvelous about the essays is that they are sharp, trenchant, satirical, in places wildly funny. She takes the prose style of an unctuous Evangelical preacher to pieces with meticulous mockery: in "Silly Novels by Lady Novelists" she writes hilarious parodies of the ridiculous plots employed by female pen-pushers and ends with a moving plea for a novel with new depths of insight. As an example of the former, here is George Eliot's description of the archetypal heroine of a species of novel she designates as *mind-and-millinery*:

> Her eyes and her wit are both dazzling; her nose and her morals are alike free from any tendency to irregularity; she has a superb *contralto* and a superb intellect; she is perfectly well-dressed and perfectly religious; she dances like a sylph and reads the Bible in the original tongues. . . . Rakish men either bite their lips in impotent confusion at her repartees,

or are touched to penitence by her reproofs; indeed there is a general propensity in her to make speeches, and to rhapsodize at some length when she retires to her bedroom. In her recorded conversations she is amazingly eloquent, and in her unrecorded conversations, amazingly witty.

At the end of the essay George Eliot produced eloquence of another order.

No educational restrictions can shut women out from the materials of fiction, and there is no species of art which is so free from rigid requirements. Like crystalline masses, it may take any form, and yet be beautiful; we have only to pour in the right elements—genuine observation, humour and passion. But it is precisely this absence of rigid requirement which constitutes the fatal seduction of novel-writing to incompetent women.

George Eliot was, I suppose, the great English novelist of ideas. By "novelist of ideas" I do not here mean novelists like Peacock, Huxley or Orwell, whose novels are dramatic presentations of beliefs they wish to mock or uphold, whose characters *represent* ideas like allegorical figures. I mean, in George Eliot's case, that she took human thought, as well as human passion, as her proper subject—*ideas*, such as thoughts on "progress," on the nature of "culture," on the growth and decay of society and societies, are as much actors in her work as the men and women who contemplate the ideas, partially understand them or unknowingly exhibit them. Part of the recent reaction against her, I suspect, is because her "ideas" have been too generally summed up as a belief in inevitable human progress, a gradual bettering of the human race, a slow movement upwards and outwards. This, with the fact that the societies she depicted were (with the notable exception of Deronda's Jewish plans for a new National Home) static, constricting, rigid in form, has led people to believe she has less to offer modern novelists than may be true.

George Eliot did indeed coin the world "meliorism" to describe a belief in gradual progress—the word is attributed to her in the OED. But she had a strong—stronger—sense of black comedy, black tragedy than she is now generally credited with, and a saving savagery in her vision of man's normal and natural inhumanity to man. She had no real heir as "novelist of ideas" in England: Lawrence's "ideas" are comparatively simple and strident, Forster's timid, and less comprehensive and forceful than hers. Her heirs are abroad—Proust in France, Mann in Germany. Which brings me to another reason for loving her: she was European, not little-English, her roots were Dante, Shakespeare, Goethe, Balzac, not just, as Leavis's Great Tradition implies, Jane Austen. She opened gates which are still open.

And I, as a woman writer, am grateful that she stands there, hidden behind the revered Victorian sage, and the Great English Tradition—a writer who could make links between mathematical skill and sexual inadequacy, between

Parliamentary Reform and a teenager's silly choice of husband, between Evangelical hypocrisy and medical advance, or its absence. When I was a girl I was impressed by John Davenport's claim, in a Sunday newspaper novel-column, that "nobody had ever really described what it felt like to be a woman." I now think that wasn't true then, and isn't true now. People are always describing that, sometimes *ad nauseam*. George Eliot did that better than most writers, too—because it was not all she did: she made a world, in which intellect and passion, day-to-day cares and movements of whole societies cohere and disintegrate. She offered us scope, not certainties. That is what I would wish to celebrate.

TONI MORRISON:
BELOVED

Beloved begins "124 was spiteful." 124 is a house in Cincinnati in 1873, inhabited by Sethe, once a runaway slave from the horribly named "Sweet Home" Kentucky farm, and her daughter, Denver. The house is spiteful because it is haunted by the terrible fury of a baby whose throat was cut to make her safe from repossession after the infamous Fugitive Slave Act. This sad ghost, possessed by infant rage and an infant's absolute and peremptory need for love, manages to materialise herself just as Sethe is cautiously attempting to come to terms with the affection offered by Paul D., the only survivor of the six "Sweet Home Men" who worked with her and loved her. Beloved—as she names herself after the one word on her pink tombstone— exacts love and payment in a wholly credible and comically disastrous way from her mother, her sister and the generous and dignified Paul D. In the early days Sethe suggested to Baby Suggs, her mother-in-law, that they move.

"What'd be the point?" asked Baby. "Not a house in the country ain't packed to its rafters with some dead Negro's grief."

If Beloved represents the terrible pain and suffering of a people whose very mother-love is warped by torture into murder, she is no thin allegory or shrill tract. This is a huge, generous, humane and gripping novel. In the foreground is the life of the black people whose courage and dignity and affection are felt to be *almost* indomitable. Their names are the no-names of non-people and are as alive as jazz with their quiddity and idiosyncrasy. Baby Sugg's owner has always believed her to be called Jenny but never asked Baby herself. The Sweet Home Men are Paul D. Garner, Paul F. Garner, Paul A. Garner, Halle Suggs and Sixo the wild man. (Garner was their owner's name: all the acknowledged individuality of Paul D.—one of the most convincing gentle adult men I have met in a book for years—resides in his D.) They do not love, or almost do not, the land whose beauty they respond to, which is not theirs, where they are not at home, though they try to make families and keep their pride. This is an adult book, but all the characters have the essential *virtue* of fairy-tale heroes and exact our primitive affection unquestioningly. Toni Morrison's love for her people is Tolstoyan in its detail and greedy curiosity; the reader is *inside* their doings and sufferings.

The world of the whites, by contrast, is almost wholly distanced—rising to the surface of consciousness only as and when the blacks can briefly bear to contemplate what it has done to them. The Civil War slips by almost without mention. Those whites who might think of themselves as good or kind are judged by Sethe's dismissive and patient acceptance of their obtuseness and ignorance about the essentials of her life. Those who whipped and tortured and hanged are judged implacably by the brief accounts of reminiscences the blacks cannot suppress, however they try to numb themselves.

The emotional condition of all the people of this story is a deliberate limitation of memory. Dying, Baby Suggs thinks "Her past had been like her present—intolerable— and since she knew death was anything but forgetfulness, she used the little energy left her for pondering color." The women do not remember the children they have borne to be sold away like fatstock, because it would hurt too much. Paul D. and Sethe, meeting after terrible years, do each other the essential courtesy of sparing themselves from their worst things, which they pass over vaguely. They do not speak of the bits and collars they have been forced to wear. But the past rises up and cries for blood like Beloved. Paul D., witched into making love to this beautiful dead thing, finds his heart, which he thinks of as a tobacco tin rusted shut, is red and alive. This living redness connects him to Baby Suggs's sermon to the black people, in which she exhorts them to love their own living bodies—neck and mouth and skin and liver and heart—since *"they"* will not.

The book is full of the colours whose absence distresses

the defeated Baby Suggs so that she hungers for yellow, or lavender, or a pink tongue even. It is also—and connectedly, through the name "colored people"—full of marvellous descriptions of the brightness and softness of black bodies—pewter skins of women skating in the cold, Sixo's indigo behind as he walks home naked after meeting his girl. Whiteness is evil and nothingness—Melville in his chapter on Whiteness in *Moby-Dick* called it "the colorless no-color from which people shrink." Beloved perceives whites as skinless. Sethe, full of rage and distress, turns on Paul D. "a look like snow."

Another profound and patterning metaphor is related to Sethe's horror when the two brutal and inhuman nephews of her schoolmaster owner write—with ink she has made for them—"a list of Sethe's animal characteristics." When Paul D. discovers what she did and attempted to do to her children in her desperation, he reproaches her, "You got two feet, not four." This image works subtly all ways. During her escape Sethe *crawls* towards the river, pregnant, desperate to reach her other unweaned baby (already in Ohio), ripped open by whipping, reduced to animal level by white man's beastliness. The child she is trying to get to—Beloved—is always described as "crawling—already?" moving on all fours and aspiring to walk straight. The slaves whose stories lie behind Toni Morrison's novel were thought by whites at this time to be in some way animal. The case for slavery was argued on these grounds. What Toni Morrison does is present an image of a people so wholly human they are almost superhuman. It is a magnificent achievement.

Toni Morrison has always been an ambitious artist, sometimes almost clotted or tangled in her own brilliant and complex vision. *Beloved* has a new strength and simplicity. This novel gave me nightmares, and yet I sat up late, paradoxically smiling to myself with intense pleasure at the exact beauty of the singing prose. It is an American masterpiece, and one which, moreover, in a curious way reassesses all the major novels of the time in which it is set. Melville, Hawthorne, Poe wrote riddling allegories about the nature of evil, the haunting of unappeased spirits, the inverted opposition of blackness and whiteness. Toni Morrison has with plainness and grace and terror—and judgment—solved the riddle, and showed us the world which haunted theirs.

COLERIDGE:
AN ARCHANGEL
A LITTLE DAMAGED

"Coleridge," said Wordsworth, "is a subject which no Biographer ought to touch beyond what he himself was eye witness of." A reading of his works—prose, poetry, letters, notebooks, marginalia—gives an impression of a personality, contradictory perhaps, but immediately impressive and to be engaged. He was plaintive and self-castigating, but nevertheless immensely alive and observant. He had a greater, more patient power to analyse the movements of thought than almost anyone else, but was always afraid he was "exercising the strength and subtlety of the understanding without awakening the feelings of the heart." He had an almost religious respect for the domestic virtues and was largely incapable of living peacefully with others. He was an enormous talker, in public and private, and a man who compelled others to talk about him; and somewhere amongst all the talk he remains a difficult and elusive figure.

Both amongst his contemporaries and amongst Coleridge students, he calls up a vigorous and contradictory mixture of judgments and reactions. After his death, Wordsworth said he was the only *wonderful* man he had ever known. There is Lamb's famous description of him reciting "Kubla Khan" in middle age: "His face hath its ancient glory; an archangel a little damaged." De Quincey's relationship with him began as passionate worship of an unknown idol—he ended by writing histrionic and vituperative attacks on Coleridge's opium-eating and his plagiarisms.

Hazlitt too began with hero-worship—to Coleridge, he said, he owed it that "my understanding did not remain dumb and brutish and at length found a language to express itself." But he wrote a series of damaging reviews of Coleridge's work, and claimed that

> Coleridge only assents to any opinion when he knows that all the reasons are against it. . . . Truth is to him a ceaseless round of contradictions: he lives in the belief of a perpetual lie, and in affecting to think what he pretends to say. . . . He would have done better if he had known less. His imagination thus becomes metaphysical, his metaphysics fantastical, his wit heavy, his arguments light, his poetry prose, his prose poetry, his politics turned—but not to account.

The mazy motion of Coleridge's walk, constantly shifting from side to side of the path, struck Hazlitt as "an odd movement; but I did not at that time connect it with any instability of purpose or involuntary change of principle as I have done since." He criticized even the poet's nose. "The rudder of the face, the index of the will, was small, feeble, nothing—like what he has done."

Modern writers repeatedly call him the greatest English critic. Coleridge scholarship goes on in an atmosphere of primary emotional and intellectual identification from sympathetic readers—not so much idolatry as passionate justification from very differing minds. But he retains his capacity to disappoint and enrage. Dr. Leavis claimed that it was scandalous that his work should be considered worthy of serious study in a university. Professor Norman Fruman's study *Coleridge the Damaged Archangel* claims with great cogency that Coleridge's deviousness, poetic and intellectual thefts and downright lying cannot be simply dismissed by anyone seeking to assess the final importance of Coleridge's work. Professor Fruman says he writes with "profound respect and a sense of deep personal affection for Coleridge," but his book is angry, and is angry rather as Hazlitt and De Quincey were angry. Respect and personal affection have been misled and betrayed.

Coleridge, of course, habitually provoked in others, and himself indulged in, these extremes of reaction to his personality. From the beginning he mocked and disparaged himself—his looks, his vacillations, even his Christian name. As a child, he wrote, he was "fretful and inordinately passionate; and as I could not play at anything and was slothful, I was despized and hated by the boys . . . before I was eight years old I was a *character*." He wrote a poem in which he mentioned his "fat vacuity of face." He was capable of using self-disparagement childishly to ingratiate himself with angry or disappointed friends. But the Journals, especially those written in Malta, during the worst days of his realisation of his enslavement to opium, express a real sharp and profound self-hatred.

On the other hand, he was aware of his own brilliance, and when he felt secure could make a public display of it in an amazing and enthralling manner. Crabb Robinson recorded his first meeting with him.

> He kept me on the stretch of attention and admiration from half-past three till 12 o'clock. On politics, metaphysics and poetry, more especially on the Regency, Kant and Shakespeare, he was astonishingly eloquent.

But Robinson found Coleridge easy to destroy in argument.

> I used afterwards to compare him as a disputant with a serpent—easy to kill if you assume the offensive, but if you let him attack, his bite is mortal. Some years after this, when I saw Mme de Stael in London, I asked her what she thought of him. That, she replied, he is very great in monologue, but he has no idea of dialogue.

There is a deeper truth in this witty judgment than is immediately apparent. Coleridge could indeed always impress with a brilliant monologue, but he was easily daunted and he was always afraid that a monologue was all it was.

He was the youngest of eight brothers and was sent away to school at the age of nine when his father died; he developed early a habit of attracting attention by impressing people, in order to mask an inner terror and loneliness. He spent his life trying to establish contacts and relationships, seeking in turn an ideal friend, an ideal community, an ideal woman, driven to expect too much and to provoke the rejection his whole history led him to recognise and anticipate. He attached himself to Robert Southey and the experimental ideal political settlement in America, the Pantisocracy; he married Southey's sister-in-law, Sara Fricker, whom he did not love, at Southey's insistence. When Southey abandoned Pantisocracy Coleridge attached himself to another friend, the wise and steady Thomas Poole at Nether Stowey, and tried to live well in rural retirement. It was at this point that he met William Wordsworth, and began what has always been seen as one of the most powerful dialogues and friendships in literary history. There followed Coleridge's wonderful year, 1797–98, in which most of his great poetry was written, and the *Lyrical Ballads* put together.

In *Biographia Literaria* Coleridge described the ideal poet as combining, among other things, "a more than usual state of emotion with much more than usual order." Much has been written about how, during this year, he was able to fuse years of disparate readings, speculations, observations, into powerfully original forms. It seems certain that without Wordsworth he might never have found this combined force of emotion and order. But the source of power was in itself a danger.

Walter Jackson Bate pointed out perceptiently that Coleridge's real sense of the nature and difficulty of true poetic achievement, combined with his great critical gifts, must have inhibited him as a poet. His ideals as well as his understanding were high. The ideal great poem should combine all human powers at their highest. In 1797 he wrote:

> I should not think of devoting less than 20 years to an Epic Poem. Ten to collect materials and warm my mind with universal science. I would be a tolerable Mathematician, I would thoroughly know Mechanics and Hydrostatics, Optics and Astronomy, Botany, Metallurgy, Fossilism, Chemistry, Geology, Anatomy, Medicine—then the *mind of man*, then the *minds of men*—in all Travels, Voyages and Histories. So I would spend ten years—the next five to the composition of the poem—and the five last to the correction of it.

The programme is inspiring and daunting; an example of Coleridge's powerful sense of the interrelated unity of all human knowledge and of an impossibly high valuation of poetic genius. Coleridge was, perhaps, historically, the last poet who could even aspire to know and work with what was known and thought about. The effect on him of his recognition of Wordsworth's genius and, later, of the very different nature of that genius from his own, is perhaps impossible finally to assess or describe. The personal relationship between the two men was for Coleridge the most intense version of his inevitable pattern of responses. Initially he identified his interests with Wordsworth's own, went to Germany, then to the Lakes with Wordsworth, devoted his time to Wordsworth's proofs and fell in love with Wordsworth's sister-in-law, Sarah Hutchinson. Later, inevitably, followed quarrels and rejection. In the early days Poole warned Coleridge of possible dangers. He retorted:

> You charge me with prostration in regard to Wordsworth. Have I affirmed anything miraculous of W? Is it impossible that a greater poet than any since Milton should appear in our days? Have any *great* poets appeared since him? . . . Future greatness! Is it not an awful thing, my dearest Poole? What if you had known Milton at the age of 30 and believed all you now know of him?

Coleridge was right about Wordsworth's greatness. But the greatness was not of the kind for which Coleridge had been preparing himself: Wordsworth did not need either the universal knowledge or the philosophical complexities or his sense of the history of literature and ideas from which Coleridge, despite his perpetual fear of losing the "natural man" in "abstruse research," drew so much energy and insight. Keats distinguished Wordsworth's poetical temperament as "the egotistical sublime": Wordsworth himself saw the great artist as "a man preferring the cultivation and exertion of his own powers in the highest possible degree to any other object of regard." Coleridge's curiosity was boundless and at his best when he lost his sense of himself in his identification with some object or set of ideas or another man's work. Both "The Ancient Mariner" and "The Leech Gatherer"—to stretch a point—are about solitary men facing extremes of human privation. Coleridge's poem is a vision: Wordsworth's, although invested with visionary dreariness, is set firmly on the earth, and is entitled "Resolution and Independence." These were precisely the qualities both men felt Coleridge lacked. During the terrible time of Coleridge's illness in the Wordsworth household, culminating in Sarah Hutchinson's departure at Wordsworth's instigation, Wordsworth repeatedly reproached Coleridge for failures in resolution and independence.

He also published, in the 1800 edition of the *Lyrical Ballads*, an ungracious note apologising for the shortcomings of "The Ancient Mariner" partly on the grounds that "the principal person has no distinct character and does not act but is continually acted upon." He complained too that "the imagery is somewhat too laboriously accumulated." Coleridge later complained of "the Wordsworths' cold praise and effective discouragement of every attempt of mine to roll onward in a distinct current of my own." But he was aware that Wordsworth's "*practical* Faith that we can do but one thing well and that therefore we must make a choice" was part of his genius, and something that he himself lacked. Wordsworth could tolerate solitude of the spirit. He could not. Yet Wordsworth was surrounded by loving and devoted women, and Coleridge himself "must not be beloved *near* him except as a satellite." At the crucial time he accepted Wordsworth's valuation of his poems with eager self-abasement, agreed to the exclusion of "Christabel" from the *Lyrical Ballads* and claimed: "I would rather have written 'Ruth' and 'Nature's Lady' than a million such poems."

To Godwin in 1801 he wrote, as though it were settled:

> The Poet is dead in me—my imagination (or rather the Somewhat that had been imaginative) lies, like a Cold Snuff on the circular Rim of a brass candlestick, without even a stink of Tallow to remind you that it was once cloath'd and mitred with Flame. . . . If I die and the Book-sellers will give you anything for my Life be sure and say—Wordsworth descended on him like the γνῶθι σε αυτὸν here from Heaven; by shewing to him what fine Poetry was, he made him know, that he himself was no Poet.

Wordsworth, initially at least, found strength in isolation, although Coleridge was arguably right when he wrote: "dear Wordsworth appears to me to have hurtfully segregated and isolated his being." In the same letter he claimed his own "many weaknesses are an advantage to me; they united me more with the great mass of my fellow-beings."

This brings us back to the crucial paradox of Coleridge's nature. He was capable himself of unique achievement in solitude, and that solitude terrified him. He was a man temperamentally condemned to create through monologue and solitary vision, who was haunted by a phantom hope of warm community, love, direct communication. His poem "Fears in Solitude" is a rather hysterical picture of the solitary contemplative who has a political vision of the close communion of Britain and the British. His "Mother Isle must be at once a son, a brother and a friend /A husband and a father." It is arguable that most of his second-rate poems and deeply felt letters strike the same extravagant note—agitated, pleasing, displaying his own insufficiencies to someone or something which *must* provide a total, harmonious response and forgiveness. His great work, on the other hand, either treats of solitary vision, or, in the case of the marvellous, intricate prose of the notebooks, has the hardness, clarity and wit of a mind contemplating in solitude, drawing strength from its own solitary activity. In the moments of strength his reality was his own inner life.

> In looking at objects of Nature while I am thinking, as at yonder moon dim-glimmering through the dewy window-pane, I seem rather to be seeking, as it were *asking*, a symbolical language for something within me that already and forever exists, than observing anything new.

It has often been said that his most persistent preoccupation was the search for unity underlying diversity. He describes the rapid associative process of his own mind with amusing brilliance but is always afraid that this mind is simply self-inclosed and self-referring. Describing in a notebook one of his own characteristic monologues, he explains that his proliferating illustrations swallow his thesis and continues:

> Psychologically my brain-fibres, or the spiritual Light which abides in the brain marrow as the visible Light appears to do in sundry rotten mackerel and other *smashy* matters, is of too general an affinity with all things, and though it perceives the *difference* of things, yet is eternally pursuing the likenesses, or rather that which is common. Bring me two things that seem the very same, and then I am quick enough to show the difference, even to hairsplitting—but to go on from circle to circle till I break against the shore of my hearer's patience, or have my concentricals dashed to nothing by a snore—this is my ordinary mishap.

He was afraid, too, that this incessant mental activity muffled the directness of his vision.

> O said I as I looked on the blue, yellow, green and purple green sea, with all its hollows and swells and cut-glass surfaces—O what an ocean of lovely forms! And I was Teazed, that the sentence sounded like a play of words. But it was not, the mind within me was struggling to express

the marvellous distinctness and unconfounded personality
of each of the million millions of forms, and yet the individual unity in which they subsisted.

Coleridge's "Dejection" ode is one of the most moving
pictures of the power and failure of the mind in solitude
that we have. Wordsworth believed that contemplation of
the powers of nature healed the human mind: Coleridge
observed the forms of the outer world, remarked, "I see,
not feel, how beautiful they are," and concluded, "I may
not hope from outward forms to win / The passion and the
life, whose fountains are within." The published poem is a
condensed, impersonal version of a long verse-letter to
Sarah Hutchinson. The verse-letter is discursive, plaintive,
self-accusing, pleading, psychologically acute and very moving. But the final Ode has gained a new power from its
compression. The contrast between the sharply observed,
almost hallucinating outer world of the poem and the passive suffering of the solitary mind is harsher and stronger
without the throbbing appeals to Sarah.

In "The Ancient Mariner," "Christabel" and "Kubla
Khan" the observed worlds have a unique glittering clarity
of extreme states of being, sunny pleasure dome, caves of
ice, burning sun, slimy sea. The central characters are passive
and suffering, unbearably isolated, waiting, at best, to revive
within themselves "that symphony and song," the vanished
passion and life whose sources are within. At his best,
Coleridge was aware that the sources of his power and his

intolerable solitude were very close together. He was like his own mariner, condemned to pluck the sleeve of the wedding guest who was returning to the human feast and community, and hold him spellbound with an almost incomprehensible monologue about the torture of the solitary spirit and its transient vision of the nature of things.

THE CHINESE LOBSTER

The proprietors of the Orient Lotus alternate frenetic embellishment with periods of lassitude and letting go. Dr. Himmelblau knows this, because she has been coming here for quick lunches, usually solitary, for the last seven years or so. She chose it because it was convenient—it is near all her regular stopping-places, the National Gallery, the Royal Academy, the British Museum—and because it seemed unpretentious and quietly comfortable. She likes its padded seats, even though the mock leather is split in places. She can stack her heavy book-bags beside her and rest her bones.

The window on to the street has been framed in struggling cheese-plants as long as she can remember. They grow denser, dustier, and still livelier as the years go by. They press their cutout leaves against the glass, the old ones holly-dark, the new ones yellow and shining. The glass distorts and folds them, but they press on. Sometimes there is a tank of coloured fish in the window, and sometimes not.

At the moment, there is not. You can see bottles of soy sauce, and glass containers which dispense toothpicks, one by one, and chrome-plated boxes full of paper napkins, also frugally dispensed one by one.

Inside the door, for the last year or so, there has been a low square shrine, made of bright jade-green pottery, inside which sits a little brass god, or sage, in the lotus position, his comfortable belly on his comfortable knees. Little lamps, and sticks of incense, burn before him in bright scarlet glass pots, and from time to time he is decorated with scarlet and gold shiny paper trappings. Dr. Himmelblau likes the colour-mixture, the bright blue-green and the saturated scarlet, so nearly the same weight. But she is a little afraid of the god, because she does not know who he is, and because he is obviously *really* worshipped, not just a decoration.

Today there is a new object, further inside the door, but still before the tables or the coathangers. It is a display-case, in black lacquered wood, standing about as high as Dr. Himmelblau's waist—she is a woman of medium height—shining with newness and sparkling with polish. It is on four legs, and its lid and sidewalls—about nine inches deep—are made of glass. It resembles cases in museums, in which you might see miniatures, or jewels, or small ceramic objects.

Dr. Himmelblau looks idly in. The display is brightly lit, and arranged on a carpet of that fierce emerald-green artificial grass used by greengrocers and undertakers.

Round the edges on opened shells is a border of raw

scallops, the pearly flesh dulling, the repeating half-moons of the orange-pink roes playing against the fierce green.

In the middle, in the very middle, is a live lobster, flanked by two live crabs. All three, in parts of their bodies, are in feeble perpetual motion. The lobster, slowly in this unbreathable element, moves her long feelers and can be seen to move her little claws on the end of her legs, which cannot go forward or back. She is black, and holds out her heavy great pincers in front of her, shifting them slightly, too heavy to lift up. The great muscles of her tail crimp and control and collapse. One of the crabs, the smaller, is able to rock itself from side to side, which it does. The crabs' mouths can be seen moving from side to side, like scissors; all three survey the world with mobile eyes still lively on little stalks. From their mouths comes a silent hissing and bubbling, a breath, a cry. The colours of the crabs are matt, brick, cream, a grape-dark sheen on the claw-ends, a dingy, earthy encrustation on the hairy legs. The lobster was, is, and will not be, blue-black and glossy. For a moment, in her bones, Dr. Himmelblau feels their painful life in the thin air. They stare, but do not, she supposes, see her. She turns on her heel and walks quickly into the body of the Orient Lotus. It occurs to her that the scallops, too, are still in some sense, probably, alive.

The middle-aged Chinese man—she knows them all well, but knows none of their names—meets her with a smile, and takes her coat. Dr. Himmelblau tells him she wants a table for two. He shows her to her usual table, and brings another bowl, china spoon, and chopsticks. The muzak starts up. Dr. Himmelblau listens with comfort and pleasure. The first time she heard the muzak, she was dismayed, she put her hand to her breast in alarm at the burst of sound, she told herself that this was not after all the peaceful retreat she had supposed. Her noodles tasted less succulent against the tin noise, and then, the second or the third time, she began to notice the tunes, which were happy, banal, Western tunes, but jazzed up and sung in what she took to be Cantonese. "Oh what a beautiful *morn*ing. Oh what a beautiful *day*. I've got a kind of a *feel*ing. Everything's *go*-ing my *way*." Only in the incomprehensible nasal syllables, against a zithery plink and plunk, a kind of gong, a sort of bell. It was not a song she had ever liked. But she has come to find it the epitome of restfulness and cheerfulness. Twang, tinkle, plink, *plink*. A cross-cultural object, an occidental Orient, an oriental Western. She associates it now with the promise of delicate savours, of warmth, of satisfaction. The middle-aged Chinese man brings her a pot of green tea, in the pot she likes, with the little transparent rice-grain flowers in the blue and white porcelain, delicate and elegant.

She is early. She is nervous about the forthcoming conversation. She has never met her guest personally, though she has of course seen him, in the flesh and on the television screen; she has heard him lecture, on Bellini, on Titian, on Mantegna, on Picasso, on Matisse. His style is orotund and idiosyncratic. Dr. Himmelblau's younger colleagues find him rambling and embarrassing. Dr. Himmel-

blau, personally, is not of this opinion. In her view, Perry
Diss is always talking about something, not about nothing,
and in her view, which she knows to be the possibly crabbed
view of a solitary intellectual, nearing retirement, this is
increasingly rare. Many of her colleagues, Gerda Himmelblau believes, do not *like* paintings. Perry Diss does. He loves
them, like sound apples to bite into, like fair flesh, like sunlight. She is thinking in his style. It is a professional hazard,
of her own generation. She has never had much style of her
own, Gerda Himmelblau—only an acerbic accuracy, which
is an *easy* style for a very clever woman who looks as though
she ought to be dry. Not arid, she would not go so far, but
dry. Used as a word of moderate approbation. She has long
fine brown hair, caught into a serviceable knot in the nape
of her neck. She wears suits in soft dark, not-quite-usual
colours—damsons, soots, black tulips, dark mosses—with
clean-cut cotton shirts, not masculine, but with no floppy
bows or pretty ribbons—also in clear colours, palest lemon,
deepest cream, periwinkle, faded flame. The suits are cut soft
but the body inside them is, she knows, sharp and angular,
as is her Roman nose and her judiciously tightened mouth.

She takes the document out of her handbag. It is not the
original, but a photocopy, which does not reproduce all
the idiosyncrasies of the original—a grease-stain, maybe
butter, here, what looks like a bloodstain, watered-down at
the edges, there, a kind of Rorschach stag-beetle made by
folding an ink-blot, somewhere else. There are also minute

drawings, in the margins and in the text itself. The whole is contained in a border of what appear to be high-arched wishbones, executed with a fine brush, in India ink. It is addressed in large majuscules

TO THE DEAN OF WOMEN STUDENTS
DR. GERDA HIMMELBLAU

and continues in minute minuscules

from peggi nollett, woman and student

It continues:

I wish to lay a formal complaint against the DISTINGUISHED VISITING PROFESSOR the Department has seen fit to appoint as the supervisor of my dissertation on The Female Body and Matisse.

In my view, which I have already made plain to anyone who cared to listen, and specificly to Doug Marks, Tracey Avison, Annie Manson, and also to you, Dr. Gerda Himmelblau, this person should never have been assigned to direct this work, as he is completley *out of* sympathy *with its feminist project. He is a so-called EXPERT on the so-called MASTER of MODERNISM but what does he know about Woman or the internal conduct of the Female Body, which has always until now been MUTE and had no mouth to speak.*

Here followed a series of tiny pencil drawings which, in the original, Dr. Himmelblau could make out to be lips, lips ambiguously oral or vaginal, she put it to herself precisely, sometimes parted, sometimes screwed shut, sometimes spattered with what might be hairs.

His criticisms of what I have written so far have always been null and extremely aggressive and destructive. He does not understand that my project is ahistorical and need not involve any description of the so-called development of Matisse's so-called style or approach, since what I wish to state is essentially critical, *and presented from a theoretical viewpoint with insights provided from contemporary critical methods to which the cronology of Matisse's life or the order in which he comitted his "paintings" is* totaly irelevant.

However although I thought I should begin by stating my theoretical position yet again I wish at the present time to lay a spercific complaint of sexual harasment *against the DVP. I can and will go into much more detail believe me Dr. Himmelblau but I will set out the gist of it so you can see there is something here* you must take up.

I am writing while still under the effect of the shock I have had so please excuse any incoherence.

It began with my usual dispirting CRIT with the DVP. He asked me why I had not writen more of the disertation than I had and I said I had not been very well and also preocupied with getting on with my art-work, as you know, in the Joint Honours Course, the creative work and the Art History get equal marks and I had reached a very difficult stage *with the Work. But I had writen some notes on Matisse's* distortions of the Female

Body with respect especially to the spercificaly Female Organs, the Breasts the Cunt the Labia etc etc and also to his ways of acumulating Flesh on certain Parts of the Body which appeal to Men and tend to imobilise Women such as grotesquely swollen Thighs or protruding Stomachs. I mean to conect this in time to the whole tradition of the depiction of Female Slaves and Odalisques but I have not yet done the research I would need to write on this.

Also his Women tend to have no features on their faces, they are Blanks, like Dolls, I find this sinister.

Anyway I told the DVP what my line on this was going to be even if I had not writen very much and he argued with me and went so far as to say I was hostile and full of hatred to Matisse. I said this was not a relevant criticism of my work and that Matisse was hostile and full of hatred towards women. He said Matisse was full of love and desire towards women (!!!!!) and I said "exactly" but he did not take the point and was realy quite cutting and undermining and dismisive and unhelpful even if no worse had hapened. He even said in his view I ought to fail my degree which is no way for a supervisor to behave as you will agree. I was so tense and upset by his atitude that I began to cry and he pated me on my shoulders and tried to be a bit nicer. So I explained how busy I was with my art-work and how my art-work, which is a series of mixed-media pieces called Erasures and Undistortions was a part of my criticism of Matisse. So he graciously said he would like to see my art-work as it might help him to give me a better grade if it contributed to my ideas on Matisse. He said art students often had dificulty expresing themselves verbally although he himself found language "as sensuous as paint." [It is not my place to say anything about his prose style but I could.] [This sentence is heavily but legibly crossed out.]

    *Anyway he came—*kindly*—to my studio to see my Work. I could see immediately he did not like it, indeed was repeled by it which I supose was not a surprise. It does not try to be agreable or seductive. He tried to put a good face on it and admired one or two* minor *pieces and went so far as to say there was a great power of feeling in the room. I tried to explain my project of* revising *or* reviewing *or* rearranging *Matisse. I have a three-dimensional piece in wire and plaster-of-paris and plasticine called* The Resistance of Madame Mattisse *which shows her and her daughter being* tortured *as they* were *by the Gestapo in the War whilst* he *sits like a Buddha cutting up pretty paper with scissors. They wouldn't tell him they were being tortured in case it disturbed his* work. *I felt sick when I found out that. The torturers have got identical scissors.*

    Then the DVP got personal. He put his arm about me and hugged me and said I had got too many clothes on. He said they were a depressing colour *and he thought I ought to take them all off and* let the air get to me. *He said he would like to see me in bright colours and that I was really a* very pretty girl *if I would let myself go. I said my clothes were a statement about myself, and he said they were a* sad statement *and then he grabed me and began kissing me and fondling me and stroking intimate parts of me—it was disgusting—I will not write it down, but I can describe it clearly, believe me Dr. Himmelblau, if it becomes necesary, I can give chapter and verse on every detail, I am still shaking with shock. The more I strugled the more he insisted and pushed at me with his body until I said I would get the police the moment he let go of me, and then he came to his senses and said that in the* good old days *painters and models felt a bit of* human warmth and sensuality *towards each other in the studio, and I said, not in my studio, and he said, clearly not, and went off, saying it seemed to him* quite likely *that I should fail both parts of my Degree.*

Gerda Himmelblau folds the photocopy again and puts it back into her handbag. She then reads the personal letter which came with it.

Dear Dr. Himmelblau,

I am sending you a complaint about a horible experience I have had. Please take it seriously and please help me. I am so unhapy, I have so little confidence in myself, I spend days and days just lying in bed wondering what is the point of geting up. I try to live for my work but I am very easily discouraged and sometimes everything seems so black and pointless it is almost hystericaly funny to think of twisting up bits of wire or modeling plasticine. Why bother I say to myself and realy there isn't any answer. I realy think I might be better off dead and after such an experience as I have just had I do slip back towards that way of thinking of thinking of puting an end to it all. The doctor at the Health Centre said just try to snap out of it what does he know? He ought to listen to people he can't realy know what individual people might do if they did snap as he puts it out of it, anyway out of what does he mean, snap out of what? The dead are snaped into black plastic sacks I have seen it on television body bags they are called. I realy think a lot about

being a body in a black bag that is what I am good for. Please help
me Dr. Himmelblau. I frighten myself and the contempt of others
is the last straw snap snap snap snap.

> *Yours sort of hopefully,*
> *Peggi Nollett.*

Dr. Himmelblau sees Peregrine Diss walk past the window
with the cheese-plants. He is very tall and very erect—
columnar, thinks Gerda Himmelblau—and has a great deal of
well-brushed white hair remaining. He is wearing an olive-
green cashmere coat with a black velvet collar. He carries a
black lacquered walking-stick, with a silver knob, which he
does not lean on, but swings. Once inside the door, observed
by but not observing Dr. Himmelblau, he studies the little
god in his green shade, and then stands and looks gravely
down on the lobster, the crabs, and the scallops. When he
had taken them in he nods to them, in a kind of respectful
acknowledgment, and proceeds into the body of the restaurant, where the younger Chinese woman takes his coat and
stick and bears them away. He looks round and sees his
host. They are the only people in the restaurant; it is early.

"Dr. Himmelblau."

"Professor Diss. Please sit down. I should have asked
whether you like Chinese food—I just thought this place
might be convenient for both of us—"

"Chinese food—well cooked, of course—is one of the
great triumphs of the human species. Such delicacy, such

intricacy, such simplicity and so *peaceful* in the aging stomach."

"I like the food here. It has certain subtleties one discovers as one goes on. I have noticed that the restaurant is frequented by large numbers of real Chinese people—families—which is always a good sign. And the fish and vegetables are always fresh, which is another."

"I shall ask you to be my guide through the plethora of the menu. I do not think I can face Fried Crispy Bowels, however much, in principle, I believe in venturing into the unknown. Are you partial to steamed oysters with ginger and spring onions? So intense, so *light* a flavour—"

"I have never had them—"

"Please try. They bear no relation to cold oysters, whatever you think of those. Which of the duck dishes do you think is the most succulent . . . ?"

They chat agreeably, composing a meal with elegant variations, a little hot flame of chilli here, a ghostly fragrant sweetness of lychee there, the salty tang of black beans, the elemental earthy crispness of beansprouts. Gerda Himmelblau looks at her companion, imagining him willy-nilly engaging in the assault described by Peggi Nollett. His skin is tanned, and does not hang in pouches or folds, although it is engraved with crisscrossing lines of very fine wrinkles absolutely all over—brows, cheeks, neck, the armature of the mouth, the eye-corners, the nostrils, the lips themselves. His eyes are a bright cornflower blue, and must, Dr. Himmelblau thinks, have been quite extraordinarily beautiful when he was a young man in the 1930s. They are still surprising, though veiled now with jelly and liquid, though bloodshot in the corners. He wears a bright cornflower-blue tie, in rough silk, to go with them, as they must have been, but also as they still are. He wears a corduroy suit, the colour of dark slate. He wears a large signet ring, lapis lazuli, and his hands, like his face, are mapped with wrinkles but still handsome. He looks both fastidious, and marked by ancient indulgence and dissipation, Gerda Himmelblau thinks, fancifully, knowing something of his history, the bare gossip, what everyone knows.

She produces the document during the first course, which is glistening viridian seaweed, and prawn and sesame toasts. She says,

"I have had this rather unpleasant letter which I must talk to you about. It seemed to me important to discuss it informally and in an unofficial context, so to speak. I don't know if it will come as a surprise to you."

Perry Diss reads quickly, and empties his glass of Tiger beer, which is quickly replaced with another by the middle-aged Chinese man.

"Poor little bitch," says Perry Diss. "What a horrible state of mind to be in. Whoever gave her the idea that she had any artistic talent ought to be shot."

Don't say bitch, Gerda Himmelblau tells him in her head, wincing.

"Do you remember the occasion she complains of?" she asks carefully.

"Well, in a way I do, in a way. Her account isn't very recognisable. We did meet last week to discuss her complete lack of progress on her dissertation—she appears indeed to have *regressed* since she put in her proposal, which I am glad to say I was *not* responsible for accepting. She has forgotten several of the meagre facts she once knew, or appeared to know, about Matisse. I do not see how she can *possibly* be given a degree—she is ignorant and lazy and pigheadedly misdirected—and I felt it my duty to tell her so. In my experience, Dr. Himmelblau, a lot of harm has been done by misguided kindness to lazy and ignorant students who have been cosseted and *nurtured* and never told they are not up to scratch."

"That may well be the case. But she make specific allegations—you went to her studio—"

"Oh yes. I went, I am not as brutal as I appear. I did try to give her the benefit of the doubt. That part of her account bears some resemblance to the truth—that is, to what I remember of those very disagreeable events. I did say something about the inarticulacy of painters and so on—you can't have worked in art schools as long as I have without knowing that some can use words and some can only use materials—it's interesting how you can't always predict *which*.

"Anyway, I went and looked at her so-called Work. The

phraseology is catching. 'So-called.' A pantechnicon contemporary term of abuse."

"And?"

"The work is *horrible*, Dr. Himmelblau. It disgusts. It desecrates. Her studio—in which the poor creature also eats and sleeps—is papered with posters of Matisse's work. *La Rêve. Le Nu rose. Le Nu bleu. Grande Robe bleue. La Musique. L'Artiste et son modèle. Zorba sur la terrasse.* And they have all been smeared and defaced. With what looks like *organic matter*—blood, Dr. Himmelblau, beef stew or faeces—I incline towards the latter since I cannot imagine good daub finding its way into that miserable tenement. Some of the daubings are deliberate reworkings of bodies or faces— changes of outlines—some are like thrown tomatoes— probable *are* thrown tomatoes—and eggs, yes—and some are *great swastikas of shit.* It is appalling. It is pathetic."

"It is no doubt meant to disgust and desecrate," states Dr. Himmelblau, neutrally.

"And what does that matter? *How can that excuse it?*" roars Perry Diss, startling the younger Chinese woman, who is lighting the wax lamps under the plate warmer, so that she jumps back.

"In recent times," says Dr. Himmelblau, "art has traditionally had an element of protest."

"*Traditional protest, hmph,*" shouts Perry Diss, his neck reddening. "Nobody minds protest, I've protested in my time, we all have, you aren't the real thing if you don't have to go at being shocking, protest is *de rigeur, I know.* But what I object to here, is the shoddiness, the laziness. It *seems to me*—forgive me, Dr. Himmelblau—but this—this *caca* offends something I do hold sacred, a word that would make that little bitch *snigger*, no doubt, but sacred, yes—it seems to me, that if she could have produced *worked copies* of those—those masterpieces—those shining—never mind—if she could have *done some work*—understood the blues, and the pinks, and the whites, and the oranges, yes, and the blacks too—and if she could still have brought herself to feel she must—must *savage* them—then I would have had to feel some respect."

"You have to be careful about the word masterpieces," murmurs Dr. Himmelblau.

"Oh, I know all that stuff, I know it well. But you have got to listen to me. It can have taken at the maximum *half an hour*—and there's no evidence anywhere in the silly girl's work that she's ever spent more than that actually *looking at* a Matisse—she has no accurate memory of one when we talk, *none*, she amalgamates them all in her mind into one monstrous female corpse bursting with male aggression—she can't *see*, can't you see? And for half an hour's shit-spreading we must give her a degree?"

"Matisse," says Gerda Himmelblau, "would sometimes make a mark, and consider, and put the canvas away for weeks or months until he *knew* where to put the next mark."

"I know."

"Well—the—the shit-spreading may have required the same consideration. As to the location of daubs."

"Don't be silly. I *can see* paintings, you know. I did look to see if there was any wit in where all this detritus was applied. Any visual *wit*, you know, I know it's meant to be funny. There wasn't. It was just slapped on. It was horrible."

"It was meant to disturb you. It disturbed you."

"Look—Dr. Himmelblau—whose side are you on? I've read your Mantegna monograph. *Mes compliments*, it is a *chef-d'oeuvre*. Have you *seen* this stuff? Have you for that matter seen Peggi Nollett?"

"I am not on anyone's *side*, Professor Diss. I am the Dean of Women Students, and I have received a formal complaint against you, about which I have to take formal action. And that could be, in the present climate, very disturbing for me, for the Department, for the University, and for yourself. I may be exceeding my strict duty in letting you know of this in this informal way. I am very anxious to know what you have to say in answer to her specific charge.

"And yes, I have seen Peggi Nollett. Frequently. And her work, on one occasion."

"Well then. If you have seen her you will know that I can have made no such—no such *advances* as she describes. Her skin is like a *potato* and her body is like a *decaying potato*, in all that great bundle of smocks and vests and knitwear and penitential hangings. Have you seen her legs and arms, Dr. Himmelblau? They are bandaged like mummies, they are all swollen with strapping and strings and then they are contained in nasty black greaves and gauntlets of plastic with buckles. You expect some awful yellow ooze to seep out between the layers, ready to be smeared on *La Joie de vivre*. And her hair, I do not think her hair can have been washed for some years. It is like a carefully preserved old frying-pan, grease undisturbed by water. You *cannot believe* I could have brought myself to touch her, Dr. Himmelblau?"

"It is difficult, certainly."

"It is impossible. I may have told her that she would be better if she wore fewer layers—I may even, imprudently—thinking, you understand, of potatoes—have said something about letting the air get to her. But I assure you that was as far as it went. I was trying against my instincts to converse with her as a human being. The rest is her horrible fantasy. I hope you will believe me, Dr. Himmelblau. You yourself are about the only almost-witness I can call in my defence."

"I do believe you," says Gerda Himmelblau, with a little sigh.

"Then let that be the end of the matter," says Perry Diss. "Let us enjoy these delicious morsels and talk about something more agreeable than Peggi Nollett. These prawns are as good as I have ever had."

"It isn't so simple, unfortunately. If she does not withdraw her complaint you will both be required to put your cases to the Senate of the University. And the University will be required—by a rule made in the days when university senates had authority and power and *money*—to retain QCs to represent both of you, should you so wish. And in the present climate I am very much afraid that whatever the truth of the matter, you will lose your job, and whether you do or don't lose it there will be disagreeable protests and demonstrations against you, your work, your continued presence in the University. And the Vice-Chancellor will fear the effect of the publicity on the funding of the College—and the course, which is the only Joint Honours Course of its kind in London—may have to close. It is *not* seen by our profit-oriented masters as an essential part of our new—'Thrust,' I think they call it. Our students do not contribute to the export drive—"

"I don't see why not. They can't *all* be Peggi Nolletts. I was about to say—have another spoonful of bamboo-shoots and beansprouts—I was about to say, very well, I'll resign on the spot and save you any further bother. But I don't think I can do that. Because I won't give in to lies and blackmail. And because that woman *isn't an artist*, and *doesn't work*, and *can't see*, and should not have a degree. And because of Matisse."

"Thank you," says Gerda Himmelblau, accepting the vegetables. And, "Oh dear yes," in response to the declaration of intent. They eat in silence for a moment or two. The Cantonese voice asserts that it is a beautiful *morn*ing. Dr. Himmelblau says,

"Peggi Nollett is not well. She is neither physically nor mentally well. She suffers from anorexia. Those clothes are designed to obscure the fact that she has starved herself, apparently, almost to a skeleton."

"Not a potato. A fork. A pin. A coathanger. I see."

"And is in a very depressed state. There have been at least two suicide bids—to my knowledge."

"Serious bids?"

"How do you define serious? Bids that would perhaps have been effective if they had not been well enough signalled—for rescue—"

"I see. You do know that this does not alter the fact that she has no talent and doesn't work, and can't see—"

"She *might*—if she were well—"

"Do you think so?"

"No. On the evidence I have, no."

Perry Diss helps himself to a final small bowlful of rice. He says,

"When I was in China, I learned to end a meal with pure rice, quite plain, and to taste every grain. It is one of the most beautiful tastes in the world, freshly-boiled rice. I don't know if it would be if it was all you had every day, if you were starving. It would be differently delicious, differently haunting, don't you think? You can't describe this taste."

Gerda Himmelblau helps herself, manoeuvres delicately with her chopsticks, contemplates pure rice, says, "I see."

"Why Matisse?" Perry Diss bursts out again, leaning forward. "I can see she is ill, poor thing. You can *smell* it on her, that she is ill. That alone makes it unthinkable that anyone—that I—should *touch* her—"

"As Dean of Women Students," says Gerda Himmelblau thoughtfully, "one comes to learn a great deal about anorexia. It appears to stem from self-hatred and inordinate self-absorption. Especially with the body, and with that image of our own body we all carry around with us. One of my colleagues who is a psychiatrist collaborated with one of your colleagues in Fine Art to produce a series of drawings—clinical drawings in a sense—which I have found most instructive. They show an anorexic person before a mirror, and what *we* see—staring ribs, hanging skin—and what *she* sees—grotesque bulges, huge buttocks, puffed cheeks. I have found these most helpful."

"Ah. *We* see coathangers and forks, and *she* sees potatoes and vegetable marrows. There is a painting in that. You could make an interesting painting out of that."

"Please—the experience is terrible to her."

"Don't think I don't know. I am not being flippant, Dr. Himmelblau. I am, or was, a serious painter. It is not flippant to see a painting in a predicament. Especially a predicament which is essentially visual, as this is."

"I'm sorry. I am trying to think *what to do*. The poor child wishes to annihilate herself. *Not to be*."

"So I understand. But *why Matisse*? If she is so obsessed with bodily horrors why does she not obtain employment as an emptier of bedpans or in a maternity ward or a hospice? And if she must take Art, why does she not rework Giacometti into Maillol, or vice versa, or take on that old goat, Picasso, who did things to women's bodies out of genuine *malice*? Why *Matisse*?"

"Precisely for that reason, as you must know. Because he paints silent bliss. *Luxe, calme et volupté*. How can Peggi Nollett bear luxe, calme et volupté?"

"When I was a young man," says Perry Diss, "going through my own Sturm und Drang, I was a bit bored by all that. I remember telling someone—my wife—it all was *easy and flat*. What a fool. And then, one day I saw it. I saw how hard it is to see, and how full of pure power, once seen. Not *consolation*, Dr. Himmelblau, *life and power*." He leans back, stares into space, and quotes,

> *"Mon enfant, ma soeur,*
> *Songe à la douceur*
> *D'aller là-bas vivre ensemble!*
> *Aimer à loisir*
> *Aimer et mourir*
> *Au pays qui te ressemble!—*
> *Là, tout n'est qu'ordre et beauté*
> *Luxe, calme et volupté."*

Dr. Himmelblau, whose own life has contained only a modicum of luxe, calme et volupté, is half-moved, half-exasperated by the vatic enthusiasm with which Perry Diss intones these words. She says drily,

"There has always been a resistance to these qualities in Matisse, of course. Feminist critics and artists don't like him because of the way in which he expands male eroticism into whole placid panoramas of well-being. Marxists don't like him because he himself said he wanted to paint to please businessmen."

"Businessmen and intellectuals," says Perry Diss.

"Intellectuals don't make it any more acceptable to Marxists."

"Look," says Perry Diss. "Your Miss Nollett wants to shock. She shocks with simple daubings. Matisse was cunning and complex and violent and controlled and *he knew he had to know exactly what he was doing.* He knew the most shocking thing he could tell people about the purpose of his art was that it was designed *to please and to be comfortable.* That sentence of his about the armchair is one of the most wickedly provocative things that has ever been said about painting. You can daub the whole of the Centre Pompidou with manure from top to bottom and you will *never* shock as many people as Matisse did by saying art was like an armchair. People remember that with horror who know nothing about the context—"

"Remind me," says Gerda Himmelblau.

"'What I dream of, is an art of balance, of purity, of quietness, without any disturbing subjects, without worry, which may be, for everyone who works with the mind, for the businessman as much as for the literary artist, something soothing, something to calm the brain, something analogous to a good armchair which relaxes him from his bodily weariness . . .'"

"It would be perfectly honourable to argue that that was a very *limited* view—" says Gerda Himmelblau.

"Honourable but impercipient. Who is it that understands *pleasure,* Dr. Himmelblau? Old men like me, who can only just remember their bones not hurting, who remember walking up a hill with a spring in their step like the red of the Red Studio. Blind men who have had their sight restored and get giddy with the colours of trees and plastic mugs and the *terrible blue* of the sky. Pleasure is *life*, Dr. Himmelblau, and most of us don't have it, or not much, or mess it up, and when we see it in those blues, those roses, those oranges, that vermilion, we should fall down and worship—for it is *the thing itself*. Who knows a good arm-chair? A man who has bone-cancer, or a man who has been tortured, he can recognise a good armchair . . ."

"And poor Peggi Nollett," says Dr. Himmelblau. "How can she see that, when she mostly wants to die?"

"Someone intent on bringing an action for rape, or what-ever she calls it, can't be all that keen on death. She will want to savour her triumph over her doddering male victim."

"She is *confused*, Professor Diss. She puts out messages of all kinds, cries for help, threats . . ."

"Disgusting art-works—"

"It is truly not beyond her capacities to—to take an overdose and leave a letter accusing you—or me—of hor-rors, of insensitivity, of persecution—"

"Vengefulness can be seen for what it is. Spite and mal-ice can be seen for what they are."

"You have a robust confidence in human nature. And you simplify. The despair is as real as the spite. They are part of each other."

"They are failures of imagination."

"Of course," says Gerda Himmelblau. "Of course they are. Anyone who could imagine the terror—the pain—of those who survive a suicide—against whom a suicide is *committed*—could not carry it through."

Her voice has changed. She knows it has. Perry Diss does not speak but looks at her, frowning slightly. Gerda Himmelblau, driven by some pact she made long ago with accuracy, with truthfulness, says,

"Of course, when one is at that point, imagining others becomes unimaginable. Everything seems clear, and simple, and *single*; there is only one possible thing to be done—"

Perry Diss says,

"That is true. You look around you and everything is bleached, and clear, as you say. You are in a white box, a white room, with no doors or windows. You are looking through clear water with no movement—perhaps it is more like being inside ice, inside the white room. There is only one thing possible. It is all perfectly clear and simple and plain. As you say."

They look at each other. The flood of red has subsided under Perry Diss's skin. He is thinking. He is quiet.

Any two people may be talking to each other, at any moment, in a civilised way about something trivial, or something, even, complex and delicate. And inside each of the two there runs a kind of dark river of unconnected thought, of secret fear, or violence, or bliss, hoped-for or lost, which keeps pace with the flow of talk and is neither seen nor heard. And at times, one or both of the two will catch sight or sound of this movement, in himself, or herself, or, more rarely, in the other. And it is like the quick slip of a waterfall into a pool, like a drop into darkness. The pace changes, the weight of the air, though the talk may run smoothly onwards without a ripple or quiver.

Gerda Himmelblau is back in the knot of quiet terror which has grown in her private self like a cancer over the last few years. She remembers, which she would rather not do, but cannot now control, her friend Kay, sitting in a heavy hospital armchair covered with mock-hide, wearing a long white hospital gown, fastened at the back, and a striped towelling dressing-gown. Kay is not looking at Gerda. Her mouth is set, her eyes are sleepy with drugs. On the white gown are scarlet spots of fresh blood, where needles have injected calm into Kay. Gerda says, "Do you remember, we are going to the concert on Thursday?" and Kay says, in a voice full of stumbling ill-will, "No, I don't, what concert?" Her eyes flicker, she looks at Gerda and away, there is something malign and furtive in her look. Gerda has loved only one person in her life, her schoolfriend, Kay. Gerda has not married, but Kay has—Gerda was bridesmaid—and Kay has brought up three children. Kay was peaceful and kindly and interested in plants, books, cakes, her husband, her children, Gerda. She was Gerda's anchor of sanity in a harsh world. As a young woman Gerda was usually described as "nervous" and also as "lucky to have Kay Leverett to keep her steady." Then one day Kay's eldest daughter was found hanging in her father's shed. A note had been left, accusing her schoolfellows of bullying. This death was not immediately the death of Kay—these things are crueller and slower. But over the years, Kay's daughter's pain became Kay's, and killed Kay. She said to Gerda once, who did not hear, who remembered only later, "I turned on the gas and lay in front of the fire all afternoon, but nothing happened." She "fell" from a window, watering a window-box. She was struck a glancing blow by a bus in the street. "I just step out now and close my eyes," she told Gerda, who said don't be silly, don't be unfair to bus-drivers. Then there was the codeine overdose. Then the sleeping-pills, hoarded with careful secrecy. And a week after Gerda saw her in the hospital chair, the success, that is to say, the real death.

The old Chinese woman clears the meal, the plates veiled with syrupy black-bean sauce, the unwanted cold rice-grains, the uneaten mange-touts.

Gerda remembers Kay saying, earlier, when her pain seemed worse and more natural, and must have been so much less, must have been bearable in a way:

"I never understood how anyone *could*. And now it seems so clear, almost the only possible thing to do, do you know?"

"No, I don't," Gerda had said, robust. "You *can't do that* to other people. You have no right."

"I suppose not," Kay had said, "but it doesn't feel like that."

"I shan't listen to you," Gerda had said. "Suicide can't be handed on."

But it can. She knows now. She is next in line. She has flirted with lumbering lorries, a neat dark figure launching herself blindly into the road. Once, she took a handful of pills, and waited to see if she would wake up, which she did, so on that day she continued, drowsily nauseated, to work as usual. She believes the impulse is wrong, to be resisted. But at the time it is white, and clear, and simple. The colour goes from the world, so that the only stain on it is her own watching mind. Which it would be easy to wipe away. And then there would be no more pain.

She looks at Perry Diss who is looking at her. His eyes are half-closed, his expression is canny and watchful. He has used her secret image, the white room, accurately; they have shared it. *He knows that she knows*, and what is more, she knows that he knows. How he knows, or when he discovered, does not matter. He has had a long life. His young wife was killed in an air-raid. He caused scandals, in his painting days, with his relations with models, with young respectable girls who had not previously been models. He was the co-respondent in a divorce case full of dirt and hatred and anguish. He was almost an important painter, but probably not quite. At the moment his work is out of fashion. He is hardly treated seriously. Like Gerda Himmelblau he carries inside himself some chamber of ice inside which sits his figure of pain, his version of kind Kay thick-spoken and malevolent in a hospital hospitality-chair.

The middle-aged Chinese man brings a plate of orange segments. They are bright, they are glistening with juice, they are packed with little teardrop sacs full of sweetness. When Perry Diss offers her the oranges she sees the old scars, well-made *efficient* scars, on his wrists. He says,

"Oranges are the real fruit of Paradise, I always think. Matisse was the first to understand orange, don't you agree? Orange in light, orange in shade, orange on blue, orange on green, orange in black—

"I went to see him once, you know, after the war, when he was living in that apartment in Nice. I was full of hope in those days, I loved him and was enraged by him and meant to outdo him, some time soon, when I had just learned this and that—which I never did. He was ill then, he had come through this terrible operation, the nuns who looked after him called him 'le ressuscité.'

"The rooms in that apartment were shrouded in darkness. The shutters were closed, the curtains were drawn. I was terribly shocked—I thought he *lived in the light*, you know, that was the idea I had of him. I blurted it out, the shock, I said, 'Oh, how can you bear to shut out the light?' And he said, quite mildly, quite courteously, that there had been some question of him going blind. He thought he had better acquaint himself with the dark. And then he added, 'and anyway, you know, black is the colour of light' Do you know the painting *La Porte noire*? It has a young woman in an armchair quite at ease in a peignoir striped in lemon and cadmium and . . . over a white dress with touches of cardinal red—her hair is yellow ochre and scarlet—and at the side is the window and the coloured light and behind—above—is the black door. Almost no one could paint the colour black as he could. Almost no one."

Gerda Himmelblau bites into her orange and tastes its sweetness. She says,

"He wrote, 'I believe in God when I work.'"

"I think he also said, 'I am God when I work.' Perhaps he is—not my God, but where—where I find that. I was brought up in the hope that I would be a priest, you know. Only I could not bear a religion which had a tortured human body hanging from the hands over its altars. No, I would rather have *The Dance*."

Gerda Himmelblau is gathering her things together. He continues,

"That is why I meant what I said, when I said that young woman's—muck-spreading—offended what I called sacred. What are we to do? I don't want her to—to punish us by self-slaughter—nor do I wish to be seen to condone the violence—the absence of *work*—"

Gerda Himmelblau sees, in her mind's eye, the face of Peggi Nollett, potato-pale, peering out of a white box with cunning, angry eyes in the slit between puffed eyelids. She sees golden oranges, rosy limbs, a voluptuously curved dark blue violin-case, in a black room. One or the other must be betrayed. Whatever she does, the bright forms will go on shining in the dark. She says,

"There is a simple solution. What she wants, what she

has always wanted, what the Department has resisted, is a sympathetic supervisor—Tracey Avison, for instance—who shares her way of looking at things—whose beliefs—who cares about political ideologies of that kind—who will—"

"Who will give her a degree and let her go on in the way she is going on. It is a defeat."

"Oh yes. It is a question of how much it matters. To you. To me. To the Department. To Peggi Nollett, too."

"It matters very much and not at all," says Perry Diss. "She may see the light. Who knows?"

They leave the restaurant together. Perry Diss thanks Dr. Himmelblau for his food and for her company. She is inwardly troubled. Something has happened to her white space, to her inner ice, which she does not quite understand. Perry Diss stops at the glass box containing the lobster, the crabs, the scallops—these last now decidedly dead, filmed with an iridescent haze of imminent putrescence. The lobster and the crabs are all still alive, all, more slowly, hissing their difficult air, bubbling, moving feet, feelers, glazing eyes. Inside Gerda Himmelblau's ribs and cranium she experiences, in a way, the pain of alien fish-flesh contracting inside an exo-skeleton. She looks at the lobster and the crabs, taking accurate distant note of the loss of gloss, the attenuation of colour.

"I find that *absolutely appalling*, you know," says Perry Diss. "And at the same time, exactly at the same time, I don't give a damn? D'you know?"

"I know," says Gerda Himmelblau. She does know. Cruelly, imperfectly, voluptuously, clearly. The muzak begins again. "*Oh* what a *beautiful morning. Oh* what a *beautiful day.*" She reaches up, in a completely uncharacteristic gesture, and kisses Perry Diss's soft cheek.

"Thank you," she says. "For everything."

"Look after yourself," says Perry Diss.

"Oh," says Gerda Himmelblau. "I will. I will."

BAGLADY

"And then," says Lady Scroop brightly, "the Company will send cars to take us all to the Good Fortune Shopping Mall. I understand that it is a real Aladdin's Cave of Treasures, where we can all find prezzies for everyone and all sorts of little indulgences for ourselves, and in perfect safety: the entrances to the Mall are under constant surveillance, sad, but necessary in these difficult days."

Daphne Gulver-Robinson looks round the breakfast table. It is beautifully laid with peach-coloured damask, bronze cutlery, and little floating gardens in lacquered dishes of waxy flowers that emit gusts of perfume. The directors of Doolittle Wind Quietus are in a meeting. Their wives are breakfasting together under the eye of Lady Scroop, the chairman's wife. It is Lord Scroop's policy to encourage his directors to travel with their wives. Especially in the Far East, and especially since the figures about AIDS began to be drawn to his attention.

Most of the wives are elegant, with silk suits and silky legs and exquisitely cut hair. They chat mutedly, swapping recipes for chutney and horror stories about nannies, staring out of the amber glass wall of the Precious Jade Hotel at the dimpling sea. Daphne Gulver-Robinson is older than most of them, and dowdier, although her husband, Rollo, has less power than most of the other directors. She has tried to make herself attractive for this jaunt and has lost ten pounds and had her hands manicured; but now she sees the other ladies, she knows it is not enough. Her style is seated tweed, and stout shoes, and bird's-nest hair.

"You don't want me on this trip," she said to Rollo when told about it. "I'd better stay and mind the donkeys and the geese and the fantails as usual, and you can have a good time, as usual, in those exotic places."

"Of course I don't want you," said Rollo. "That is, of course I *want* you, but I do know you're happier with the geese and the donkeys and pigs and things. But Scroop will think it's very odd, *I'm* very odd, if you don't come. He gets bees in his bonnet. You'll like the shopping; the ladies do a lot of shopping, I believe. You might like the other wives," he finished, not hopefully.

"I didn't like boarding-school," Daphne said.

"I don't see what that has to do with it," Rollo said. There is a lot Rollo doesn't see. Doesn't want to see and doesn't see.

Lady Scroop tells them they may scatter in the Mall as much as they like as long as they are all back at the front entrance at noon precisely. "We have all *packed our bags*, I hope," she says, "though I have left time on the schedule for adjustments to make space for any goodies we may find. And then there will be a *delicious lunch* at the Pink Pearl Café and then we leave at two-forty-five *sharp* for the airport and on to Sydney."

The ladies pack into the cars. Daphne Gulver-Robinson is next to the driver of her Daimler, a place of both comfort and isolation. They swoop silently through crowded streets, isolated by bullet-proof glass from the smells and sounds of the Orient. The Mall is enormous and not beautiful. Some of the ladies have been in post-modern pink and peppermint Malls in San Diego, some have been in snug, glittering underground tunnels in Canadian winters, some have shopped in crystal palaces in desert landscapes, with tinkling fountains and splashing streams. The Good Fortune Shopping Mall resembles an army barracks or a prison block, but it is not for the outside they have come, and they hasten to trip inside, like hens looking for worms, jerking and clucking, Daphne Gulver-Robinson thinks malevolently, as none of them waits for her.

She synchronises her watch with the driver, and goes in alone, between the sleepy soldiers with machine-guns and the uniformed police with their revolvers and little sticks. Further away, along the walls of the Mall, are little groups and gangs of human flotsam and jetsam, gathered with bags and bottles around little fires of cowdung or cardboard. There is a no-man's-land, swept clean, between them and the police.

She is not sure she likes shopping. She looks at her watch, and wonders how she will fill the two hours before the rendezvous. She walks rather quickly past rows of square shop-fronts, glittering with gilt and silver, shining with pearls and opals, shimmering with lacquer and silk. Puppets and shadow-puppets mop and mow, paper birds hop on threads, paper dragons and monstrous goldfish gape and dangle. She covers the first floor, or one rectangular arm of the first floor, ascends a flight of stairs and finds herself on another floor, more or less the same, except for a few windows full of sober suiting, a run of American-style T-shirts, an area of bonsai trees. She stops to look at the trees, remembering her garden, and thinks of buying a particularly shapely cherry. But how could it go to Sydney, how return to Norfolk, would it even pass customs?

She has slowed down now and starts looking. She comes to a corner, gets into a lift, goes up, gets out, finds herself on a higher, sunnier, emptier floor. There are fewer shoppers. She walks along one whole "street" where she is the only shopper, and is taken by a display of embroidered silk cushion-covers. She goes in, and turns over a heap of about a hundred, quick, quick, chrysanthemums, cranes, peach-blossom, blue-tits, mountain tops. She buys a cover with a circle of embroidered fish, red and gold and copper, because it is the only one of its kind, perhaps a rarity.

When she looks in her shopping bag, she cannot find her camera, although she is sure it was there when she set out. She buys a jade egg on the next floor, and some lacquered chopsticks, and a mask with a white furious face for her student daughter. She is annoyed to see a whole window full of the rare fishes, better embroidered than the one in the bag. She follows a sign saying CAFÉ but cannot find the café, though she trots on, faster now. She does find a ladies' room, with cells so small they are hard to squeeze into. She restores her make-up there: she looks hot and blowzy. Her lipstick has bled into the soft skin round her mouth. Hair-pins have sprung out. Her nose and eyelids shine. She looks at her watch, and thinks she should be making her way back to the entrance. Time has passed at surprising speed.

Signs saying EXIT appear with great frequency and lead to fire-escape-like stairways and lifts, which debouch only in identical streets of boxed shop-fronts. They are designed, she begins to think, to keep you inside, to direct you past even more shops, in seach of a hidden, deliberately elusive way out. She runs a little, trotting quicker, toiling up concrete stairways, clutching her shopping. On one of these stairways a heel breaks off one of her smart shoes. After a moment she takes off both, and puts them in her shopping bag. She hobbles on, on the concrete, sweating and panting. She dare not look at her watch, and then does. The time of the rendezvous is well past. She thinks she might call the hotel, opens her handbag, and finds that her purse and credit cards have mysteriously disappeared.

There is nowhere to sit down: she stands in the Mall, going through and through her handbag, long after it is clear that the things have vanished. Other things, dislodged, have to be retrieved from the dusty ground. Her fountain-pen has gone too, Rollo's present for their twentieth wedding anniversary. She begins to run quite fast, so that huge holes spread in the soles of her stockings, which in the end split, and begin to work their way over her feet and up her legs in wrinkles like flaking skin. She looks at her watch; the packing-time and the "delicious lunch" are over: it is almost time for the airport car. Her bladder is bursting, but she *must go on*, and must go *down*, the entrance is down.

It is in this way that she discovers that the Good Fortune Mall extends maybe as far into the earth as into the sky, excavated identical caverns of shopfronts, jade, gold, silver, silk, lacquer, watches, suiting, bonsai trees and masks and puppets. Lifts that say they are going down go only up. Stairwells are windowless: ground level cannot be found. The plane has now taken off with or without the directors and ladies of Doolittle Wind Quietus. She takes time out in another concrete and stainless-steel lavatory cubicle, and then looks at the watch, whose face has become a whirl of terror. Only now it is merely a compressed circle of pink skin, shiny with sweat. Her watch, too, has gone. She utters faint little moaning sounds, and then an experimental scream. No one appears to hear or see her, neither strolling shoppers, deafened by Walkmans or by propriety, or by fear of the strange, nor shopkeepers, watchful in their cells.

Nevertheless, screaming helps. She screams again, and then screams and screams into the thick, bustling silence. A man in a brown overall brings a policeman in a reinforced hat, with a gun and a stick.

"Help me," says Daphne. "I am an English lady, I have been robbed, I must get home."

"Papers," says the policeman.

She looks in the back pocket of her handbag. Her passport, too, has gone. There is nothing. "Stolen. All stolen," she says.

"People like you," says the policeman, "not allowed in here."

She sees herself with his eyes, a baglady, dirty, unkempt, with a bag full of somebody's shopping, a tattered battery-hen.

"My husband will come and look for me," she tells the policeman.

If she waits, if she stays in the Mall, he will, she thinks. He *must*. She sees herself sitting with the flotsam and jetsam beyond the swept no-man's-land, outside.

"I'm not moving," she says, and sits down heavily. She has to stay in the Mall. The policeman prods her with his little stick.

"Move, please."

It is more comfortable sitting down.

"I shall stay here forever if necessary," she says.

She cannot imagine anyone coming. She cannot imagine getting out of the Good Fortune Mall.

CHRIST IN THE HOUSE OF
MARTHA AND MARY

Cooks are notoriously irascible. The new young woman, Dolores, was worse than most, Concepción thought. Worse and better, that was. She had an extraordinary fine nose for savours and spices, and a light hand with pastries and batters, despite her stalwart build and her solid arms. She could become a true artist, if she chose, she could go far. But she didn't know her place. She sulked, she grumbled, she complained. She appeared to think it was by some sort of unfortunate accident that she had been born a daughter of servants, and not a delicate lady like Doña Conchita who went to church in sweeping silks and a lace veil. Concepción told Dolores, not without an edge of unkindness, that she wouldn't look so good in those clothes, anyway. You are a mare built for hard work, not an Arab filly, said Concepción. You are no beauty. You are all brawn, and you should thank God for your good health in the station to which he has called you. Envy is a deadly sin.

It isn't envy, said Dolores. I want to live. I want time to think. Not to be pushed around. She studied her face in a shining copper pan, which exaggerated the heavy cheeks, the angry pout. It was true she was no beauty, but no woman likes being told so. God had made her heavy, and she hated him for it.

The young artist was a friend of Concepción's. He borrowed things, a pitcher, a bowl, a ladle, to sketch them over and over. He borrowed Concepción, too, sitting quietly in a corner, under the hooked hams and the plaits of onions and garlic, and drawing her face. He made Concepción look, if not ideally beautiful, then wise and graceful. She had good bones, a fine mouth, a wonderful pattern of lines on her brow and etched beside her nose, which Dolores had not been interested in until she saw the shapes he made from them. His sketches of Concepción increased her own knowledge that she was not beautiful. She never spoke to him, but worked away in a kind of fury in his presence, grinding the garlic in the mortar, filleting the fish with concentrated skill, slapping dough, making a tattoo of sounds with the chopper, like hailstones, reducing onions to fine specks of translucent light. She felt herself to be a heavy space of unregarded darkness, a weight of miserable shadow in the corners of the room he was abstractedly recording. He had given Concepción an oil painting he had made, of shining fish and white solid eggs, on a chipped earthenware dish. Dolores did not know why this painting moved her. It was silly that oil paint on board should make eggs and fish more real, when they were less so. But it did. She never spoke to him, though she partly knew that if she did, he might in the end give her some small similar patch of light in darkness to treasure.

Sunday was the worst day. On Sunday, after Mass, the family entertained. They entertained family and friends, the priest and sometimes the bishop and his secretary, they sat and conversed, and Doña Conchita turned her dark eyes and her pale, long face to listen to the Fathers, as they made kindly jokes and severe pronouncements on the state of the nation, and of Christendom. There were not enough servants to keep up the flow of sweetmeats and pasties, syllabubs and jellies, quails and tartlets, so that Dolores was sometimes needed to fetch and carry as well as serve, which she did with an ill grace. She did not cast her eyes modestly down, as was expected, but stared around her angrily, watching the convolutions of Doña Conchita's neck with its pretty necklace, the tapping of her pretty foot, directed not at the padre whose words she was demurely attending to, but at young Don José on the other side of the room. Dolores put a hot dish of peppers in oil down on the table with such force that the pottery burst apart, and oil and spices ran into the damask cloth. Doña Ana, Doña Conchita's governess, berated Dolores for a whole minute, threatening dismissal, docking of wages, not only for clumsiness but for insolence. Dolores strode back into the kitchen, not slinking, but moving her large legs like walking oak trees, and began to shout. There was no need to dismiss her, she was off. This was no life for a human being. She was no worse than *they* were, and more of use. She was off.

The painter was in his corner, eating her dish of elvers and *alioli*. He addressed her directly for the first time, remarking that he was much in her debt, over these last weeks, for her good nose for herbs, for her tact with sugar and spice, for her command of sweet and sour, rich and delicate. You are a true artist, said the painter, gesturing with his fork.

Dolores turned on him. He had no right to mock her, she said. He was a true artist, he could reveal light and beauty in eggs and fishes that no one had seen, and which they would then always see. She made pastries and dishes that went out of the kitchen beautiful and came back man-gled and mashed—they don't notice what they're eating, they're so busy talking, and they don't eat most of it, in case they grow fat, apart from the priests, who have no other pleasures. They order it all for show, for show, and it lasts a minute only until they put the knife to it, or push it around their plate elegantly with a fork.

The painter put his head on one side, and considered her red face as he considered the copper jugs, or the glass-ware, narrowing his eyes to a slit. He asked her if she knew the story St. Luke told, of Christ in the house of Martha and Mary. No, she said, she did not. She knew her catechism, and what would happen to sinners at the Last Judgment, which was on the wall of the church. And about butchered martyrs, who were also on the walls of the church.

They were sisters, the painter told her, who lived in Bethany. Jesus visited them, from time to time, and rested there. And Mary sat at his feet and listened to his words, and Martha was cumbered with much serving, as St. Luke put it, and complained. She said to the Lord, "Dost thou not care that my sister hath left me to serve alone? Bid her therefore that she help me." And Jesus said to her, "Martha, Martha, thou art careful and troubled about many things: but one thing is needful, and Mary hath chosen that good part, which shall not be taken away from her."

Dolores considered this, drawing her brows together in an angry frown. She said, "There speaks a man, for certain. There will always be serving, and someone will always be doomed to serving, and will have no choice or chance about the *better part*. Our Lord could make loaves and fishes from the air for the listeners, but mere mortals cannot. So we—Concepción and I—serve them whilst they have the *better part* they have chosen."

And Concepción said that Dolores should be careful, or she would be in danger of blaspheming. She should learn to accept the station the Lord had given her. And she appealed to the painter, should Dolores not learn to be content, to be patient? Hot tears sprang in Dolores's eyes. The painter said:

"By no means. It is not a question of accepting our station in the world as men have ordered it, but of learning not to be careful and troubled. Dolores here has her way to that better part, even as I have, and, like mine, it begins in attention to loaves and fishes. What matters is not that silly girls push her work about their plates with a fork, but that the work is good, that she understands what the wise understand, the nature of garlic and onions, butter and oil, eggs and fish, peppers, aubergines, pumpkins and corn. The cook, as much as the painter, looks into the essence of the creation, not, as I do, in light and on surfaces, but with all the other senses, with taste, and smell, and touch, which God also made in us for purposes. You may come at the *better part* by understanding emulsions, Dolores, by studying freshness and the edges of decay in leaves and flesh, by mixing wine and blood and sugar into sauces, as well as I may, and likely better than fine ladies twisting their pretty necks so that the light may catch their pretty pearls. You are very young, Dolores, and very strong, and very angry. You must learn *now*, that the important lesson—as long as you have your health—is that the divide is not between the servants and the served, between the leisured and the workers, but between those who are *interested* in the world and its multiplicity of forms and forces, and those who merely subsist, worrying or yawning. When I paint eggs and fishes and onions, I am painting the godhead—not only because eggs have been taken as an emblem of the Resurrection, as have dormant roots with green shoots, not only because the letters of Christ's name make up the Greek word for fish, but because the world is full of light and life, and the true crime is not to be interested in it. You have a way in. Take it. It may incidentally be a way out, too, as all skills are. The Church teaches that Mary is the contemplative life, which is higher than Martha's way, which is the active way. But any painter must question, which is which? And a cook also contemplates mysteries."

"I don't know," said Dolores, frowning. He tilted his head the other way. Her head was briefly full of images of the skeletons of fishes, of the whirlpool of golden egg-and-oil in the bowl, of the pattern of muscles in the shoulder of a goat. She said, "It is nothing, what I know. It is past in a flash. It is cooked and eaten, or it is gone bad and fed to the dogs, or thrown out."

"Like life," said the painter. "We eat and are eaten, and we are very lucky if we reach our three score years and ten, which is less than a flash in the eyes of an angel. The understanding persists, for a time. In your craft and mine."

He said, "Your frown is a powerful force in itself. I have an idea for a painting of Christ in the house of Martha and Mary. Would you let me draw you? I have noticed that you were unwilling."

"I am not beautiful."

"No. But you have power. Your anger has power, and you have power yourself, beyond that."

She had the idea, then, over the weeks and months when he visited from time to time and sketched her, and Concepción, or ate the *alioli* and supped her red peppers and raisins, praising the flavours, that he would make her heroic, a kind of goddess wielding spit and carving knife instead of spear and sword. She found herself posing, saw him noting the posing, and tried to desist. His interest in the materials of her art did indeed fire her own interest in them. She excelled herself, trying new combinations for him, offering new juices, frothing new possets. Concepción was afraid that the girl would fall in love with the artist, but in some unobtrusively clever way he avoided that. His slit stare, his compressed look of concentration, were the opposite of erotic. He talked to the girl as though she were a colleague, a partner in the mystery of his trade, and this, Concepción saw without wholly knowing that she saw it, gave Dolores a dignity, a presence, that amorous attentions would not have done. He did not show the women the sketches of themselves, though he gave them small drawings of heads of garlic and long capsicum to take to their rooms. And when, finally, the painting of *Christ in the House of Martha and Mary* was finished, he invited both women to come and look at it in his studio. He seemed, for the first time, worried about their reaction.

When they saw the painting, Concepción drew in her breath. There they both were, in the foreground at the left. She herself was admonishing the girl, pointing with a

raised finger to the small scene at the top right-hand corner of the painting—was it through a window, or over a
sill, or was it an image of an image on a wall? it was not
clear—where Christ addressed the holy staring woman
crouched at his feet whilst her sister stood stolidly behind,
looking also like Concepción, who had perhaps modelled
for her from another angle. But the light hit four things—
the silvery fish, so recently dead that they were still bright-
eyed, the solid white gleam of the eggs, emitting light, the
heads of garlic, half-peeled and life-like, and the sulky, fleshy,
furiously frowning face of the girl, above her fat red arms
in their brown stuff sleeves. He had immortalised her ugli-
ness, Concepción thought, she would never forgive him. She
was used to paintings of patient and ethereal Madonnas. This
was living flesh, in a turmoil of watchful discontent. She
said, "Look how real the eyes of the fishes are," and her
voice trailed foolishly away, as she and the painter watched
the live Dolores watch her image.

She stood and stared. She stared. The painter shifted from
foot to foot. Then she said, "Oh yes, I see what you saw,
how very strange." She said, "How very strange, to have been
looked at so intently." And then she began to laugh. When
she laughed, all the down-drooping lines of cheek and lip
moved up and apart. The knit brows sprang apart, the eyes
shone with amusement, the young voice pealed out. The
momentary coincidence between image and woman vanished, as though the rage was still and eternal in the paint-

ing and the woman was released into time. The laughter was infectious, as laughter is; after a moment Concepción, and then the painter, joined in. He produced wine, and the women uncovered the offering they had brought, spicy tortilla and salad greens. They sat down and ate together.

THE THING IN THE FOREST

There were once two little girls who saw, or believed they saw, a thing in a forest. The two little girls were evacuees, who had been sent away from the city by train, with a large number of other children. They all had their names attached to their coats with safety-pins, and they carried little bags or satchels, and the regulation gas-mask. They wore knitted scarves and bonnets or caps, and many had knitted gloves attached to long tapes which ran along their sleeves, inside their coats, and over their shoulders and out, so that they could leave their ten woollen fingers dangling, like a spare pair of hands, like a scarecrow. They all had bare legs and scuffed shoes and wrinkled socks. Most had wounds on their knees in varying stages of freshness and scabbiness. They were at the age when children fall often and their knees were unprotected. With their suitcases, some of which were almost too big to carry, and their other impedimenta, a doll, a toy car, a comic, they were like a disorderly dwarf regiment, stomping along the platform.

The two little girls had not met before, and made friends on the train. They shared a square of chocolate, and took alternate bites at an apple. One gave the other the inside page of her *Beano*. Their names were Penny and Primrose. Penny was thin and dark and taller, possibly older, than Primrose, who was plump and blonde and curly. Primrose had bitten nails, and a velvet collar to her dressy green coat. Penny had a bloodless transparent paleness, a touch of blue in her fine lips. Neither of them knew where they were going, nor how long the journey might take. They did not even know why they were going, since neither of their mothers had quite known how to explain the danger to them. How do you say to your child, I am sending you away, because enemy bombs may fall out of the sky, because the streets of the city may burn like forest fires of brick and timber, but I myself am staying here, in what I believe may be daily danger of burning, burying alive, gas, and ultimately perhaps a grey army rolling in on tanks over the suburbs, or sailing its submarines up our river, all guns blazing? So the mothers (who did not resemble each other at all) behaved alike, and explained nothing, it was easier. Their daughters they knew were little girls, who would not be able to understand or imagine.

The girls discussed on the train whether it was a sort of holiday or a sort of punishment, or a bit of both. Penny had read a book about Boy Scouts, but the children on the train did not appear to be Brownies or Wolf Cubs, only a mongrel battalion of the lost. Both little girls had the idea that these were all perhaps *not very good* children, possibly being sent away for that reason. They were pleased to be able to define each other as "nice." They would stick together, they agreed. Try to sit together, and things.

The train crawled sluggishly further and further away from the city and their homes. It was not a clean train—the upholstery of their carriage had the dank smell of unwashed trousers, and the gusts of hot steam rolling backwards past their windows were full of specks of flimsy ash, and sharp grit, and occasional fiery sparks that pricked face and fingers like hot needles if you opened the window. It was very noisy too, whenever it picked up a little speed. The engine gave great bellowing sighs, and the invisible wheels underneath clicked rhythmically and monotonously, tap-tap-tap-CRASH, tap-tap-tap-CRASH. The window-panes were both grimy and misted up. The train stopped frequently, and when it stopped, they used their gloves to wipe rounds, through which they peered out at flooded fields, furrowed hillsides and tiny stations whose names were carefully blacked out, whose platforms were empty of life.

The children did not know that the namelessness was meant to baffle or delude an invading army. They felt—they did not think it out, but somewhere inside them the idea sprouted—that the erasure was because of them, because they were not meant to know where they were going or, like Hansel and Gretel, to find the way back. They did not speak to each other of this anxiety, but began the kind of conversation children have about things they really disliked, things that upset, or disgusted, or frightened them. Semolina pudding with its grainy texture, mushy peas, fat on roast meat. Listening to the stairs and the window-sashes creaking in the dark or the wind. Having your head held roughly back over the basin to have your hair washed, with cold water running down inside your liberty bodice. Gangs in playgrounds. They felt the pressure of all the other alien children in all the other carriages as a potential gang. They shared another square of chocolate, and licked their fingers, and looked out at a great white goose flapping its wings beside an inky pond.

The sky grew dark grey and in the end the train halted. The children got out, and lined up in a crocodile, and were led to a mud-coloured bus. Penny and Primrose managed to get a seat together, although it was over the wheel, and both of them began to feel sick as the bus bumped along snaking country lanes, under whipping branches, dark leaves on dark wooden arms on a dark sky, with torn strips of thin cloud streaming across a full moon, visible occasionally between them.

They were billeted temporarily in a mansion commandeered from its owner, which was to be arranged to hold a hospital for the long-term disabled, and a secret store of artworks and other valuables. The children were told they were there temporarily, until families were found to take them all into their homes. Penny and Primrose held hands, and said to each other that it would be wizard if they could go to the same family, because at least they would have each other. They didn't say anything to the rather tired-looking ladies who were ordering them about, because with the cunning of little children, they knew that requests were most often counter-productive, adults liked saying no. They imagined possible families into which they might be thrust. They did not discuss what they imagined, as these pictures, like the black station signs, were too fright-ening, and words might make some horror solid, in some magical way. Penny, who was a reading child, imagined Victorian dark pillars of severity, like Jane Eyre's Mr. Brocklehurst, or David Copperfield's Mr. Murdstone. Prim-rose imagined—she didn't know why—a fat woman with a white cap and round red arms who smiled nicely but made the children wear sacking aprons and scrub the steps and the stove. "It's like we were orphans," she said to Penny. "But we're not," Penny said. "If we manage to stick together . . ."

The great house had a double flight of imposing stairs to its front door, and carved griffins and unicorns on its balus-trade. There was no lighting, because of the black-out. All the windows were shuttered. No welcoming brightness leaked across door or windowsill. The children trudged up

the staircase in their crocodile, hung their coats on num-
bered makeshift hooks, and were given supper (Irish stew
and rice pudding with a dollop of blood-red jam) before
going to bed in long makeshift dormitories, where once servants had slept. They had camp-beds (military issue) and
grey shoddy blankets. Penny and Primrose got beds together
but couldn't get a corner. They queued to brush their teeth
in a tiny washroom, and both suffered (again without speaking) suffocating anxiety about what would happen if they
wanted to pee in the middle of the night, because the lavatory was one floor down, the lights were all extinguished,
and they were a long way from the door. They also suffered
from a fear that in the dark the other children would start
laughing and rushing and teasing, and turn themselves into
a gang. But that did not happen. Everyone was tired and
anxious and orphaned. An uneasy silence, a drift of per-
turbed sleep, came over them all. The only sounds—from all
parts of the great dormitory it seemed—were suppressed
snuffles and sobs, from faces pressed into thin pillows.

When daylight came, things seemed, as they mostly do,
brighter and better. The children were given breakfast in a
large vaulted room. They sat at trestle tables, eating porridge made with water and a dab of the red jam, heavy
cups of strong tea. Then they were told they could go out
and play until lunch-time. Children in those days—wherever
they came from—were not closely watched, were allowed
to come and go freely, and those evacuated children were
not herded into any kind of holding-pen, or transit camp.

They were told they should be back for lunch at 12:30, by which time those in charge hoped to have sorted out their provisional future lives. It was not known how they would know when it was 12:30, but it was expected that—despite the fact that few of them had wrist-watches—they would know how to keep an eye on the time. It was what they were used to.

Penny and Primrose went out together, in their respectable coats and laced shoes, on to the terrace. The terrace appeared to them to be vast, and was indeed extensive. It was covered with a fine layer of damp gravel, stained here and there bright green, or invaded by mosses. Beyond it was a stone balustrade, with a staircase leading down to a lawn, which that morning had a quicksilver sheen on the lengthening grass. It was flanked by long flower-beds, full of overblown annuals and damp clumps of stalks. A gardener would have noticed the beginnings of neglect, but these were urban little girls, and they noticed the jungly mass of wet stems, and the wet, vegetable smell. Across the lawn, which seemed considerably vaster than the vast terrace, was a sculpted yew hedge, with many twigs and shoots out of place and ruffled. In the middle of the hedge was a wicket-gate, and beyond the gate were trees, woodland, a forest, the little girls said to themselves.

"Let's go into the forest," said Penny, as though the sentence was required of her.

Primrose hesitated. Most of the other children were running up and down the terrace, scuffing their shoes in the gravel. Some boys were kicking a ball on the grass. The sun came right out, full from behind a hazy cloud, and the trees suddenly looked both gleaming and secret.

"OK," said Primrose. "We needn't go far."

"No. I've never been in a forest."

"Nor me."

"We ought to look at it, while we've got the opportunity," said Penny.

There was a very small child—one of the smallest—whose name, she told everyone, was Alys. With a y, she told those who could spell, and those who couldn't, which surely included herself. She was barely out of nappies. She was quite extraordinarily pretty, pink and white, with large pale blue eyes, and sparse little golden curls all over her head and neck, through which her pink skin could be seen. Nobody seemed to be in charge of her, no elder brother or sister. She had not quite managed to wash the tearstains from her dimpled cheeks.

She had made several attempts to attach herself to Penny and Primrose. They did not want her. They were excited about meeting and liking each other. She said now:

"I'm coming too, into the forest."

"No, you aren't," said Primrose.

"You're too little, you must stay here," said Penny.

"You'll get lost," said Primrose.

"You won't get lost. I'll come with you," said the little creature, with an engaging smile, made for loving parents and grandparents.

"We don't want you, you see," said Primrose.

"It's for your own good," said Penny.

Alys went on smiling hopefully, the smile becoming more of a mask.

"It will be all right," said Alys.

"Run," said Primrose.

They ran; they ran down the steps and across the lawn, and through the gate, into the forest. They didn't look back. They were long-legged little girls, not toddlers. The trees were silent round them, holding out their branches to the sun, breathing noiselessly.

Primrose touched the warm skin of the nearest saplings, taking off her gloves to feel their cracks and knots. She exclaimed over the flaking whiteness and dusty brown of the silver birches, the white leaves of the aspens. Penny looked into the thick of the forest. There was undergrowth—a mat of brambles and bracken. There were no obvious paths. Dark and light came and went, inviting and mysterious, as the wind pushed clouds across the face of the sun.

"We have to be careful not to get lost," she said. "In stories, people make marks on tree-trunks, or unroll a thread, or leave a trail of white pebbles—to find their way back."

"We needn't go out of sight of the gate," said Primrose. "We could just explore a little bit."

They set off, very slowly. They went on tiptoe, making their own narrow passages through the undergrowth, which sometimes came as high as their thin shoulders. They were urban, and unaccustomed to silence. At first the absence of human noise filled them with a kind of awe, as though, while they would not have put it to themselves in this way, they had got to some original place, from which they, or those before them, had come, and which they therefore recognised. Then they began to hear the small sounds that were there. The chatter and repeated lilt and alarm of invisible birds, high up, further in. The hum and buzz of insects. Rustling in dry leaves, rushes of movement in thickets. Slitherings, dry coughs, sharp cracks. They went on, pointing out to each other creepers draped with glistening berries, crimson, black and emerald, little crops of toadstools, some scarlet, some ghostly-pale, some a dead-flesh purple, some like tiny parasols—and some like pieces of meat protruding from tree-trunks. They met blackberries, but didn't pick them, in case in this place they were dangerous or deceptive. They admired from a safe distance the stiff upright fruiting rods of the Lords and Ladies, packed with fat red berries. They stopped to watch spiders spin, swinging from twig to twig, hauling in their silky cables, reinforcing knots and joinings. They sniffed the air, which was full of a warm mushroom smell, and a damp moss smell, and a sap smell, and a distant hint of dead ashes.

Did they hear it first or smell it first? Both sound and scent were at first infinitesimal and dispersed. Both gave the strange impression of moving in—in waves—from the whole perimeter of the forest. Both increased very slowly in volume, and both were mixed, a sound and a smell fabricated of many disparate sounds and smells. A crunching, a crackling, a crushing, a heavy thumping, combined with threshing and thrashing, and added to that a gulping, heaving, boiling, bursting steaming sound, full of bubbles and farts, piffs and explosions, swallowings and wallowings. The smell was worse, and more aggressive, than the sound. It was a liquid smell of putrefaction, the smell of maggoty things at the bottom of untended dustbins, the smell of blocked drains, and unwashed trousers, mixed with the smell of bad eggs, and of rotten carpets and ancient polluted bedding. The new, ordinary forest smells and sounds, of leaves and humus, fur and feathers, so to speak, went out like lights as the atmosphere of the thing preceded it. The two little girls looked at each other, and took each other's hand. Speechlessly and instinctively they crouched down behind a fallen tree-trunk, and trembled, as the thing came into view.

Its head appeared to form, or become first visible in the distance, between the trees. Its face—which was triangular—appeared like a rubbery or fleshy mask over a shapeless sprouting bulb of a head, like a monstrous turnip. Its colour was the colour of flayed flesh, pitted with wormholes, and its expression was neither wrath nor greed, but pure misery. Its most defined feature was a vast mouth, pulled down and down at the corners, tight with a kind of pain. Its lips were thin, and raised, like welts from whipstrokes. It had blind, opaque white eyes, fringed with fleshy lashes and brows like the feelers of sea-anemones. Its face was close to the ground, and moved towards the children between its forearms which were squat, thick, powerful and akimbo, like a cross between a monstrous washerwoman and a primeval dragon. The flesh on these forearms was glistening and mottled, every colour, from the green of mould to the red-brown of raw liver, to the dirty white of dry rot.

The rest of its very large body appeared to be glued together, like still-wet papier-mâché, or the carapace of stones and straws and twigs worn by caddis-flies underwater. It had a tubular shape, as a turd has a tubular shape, a provisional amalgam. It was made of rank meat, and decaying vegetation, but it also trailed veils and prostheses of man-made materials, bits of wire-netting, foul dishcloths, wire-wool full of panscrubbings, rusty nuts and bolts. It had feeble stubs and stumps of very slender legs, growing out of it at all angles, wavering and rippling like the suckered feet of a caterpillar or the squirming fringe of a centipede. On and on it came, bending and crushing whatever lay in its path, including bushes, though not substantial trees, which it wound between, awkwardly. The little girls observed, with horrified fascination, that when it met a sharp stone, or a narrow tree-trunk, it allowed itself to be sliced through, flowed sluggishly round in two or three smaller worms, convulsed and reunited. Its progress was achingly slow, very smelly, and apparently very painful, for it moaned and whined amongst its other burblings and belchings. They thought it could not see, or certainly could not see clearly. It and its stench passed within a few feet of their tree-trunk, humping along, leaving behind it a trail of bloody slime and dead foliage, sucked to dry skeletons.

Its end was flat and blunt, almost transparent, like some earthworms.

When it had gone, Penny and Primrose, kneeling on the moss and dead leaves, put their arms about each other, and hugged each other, shaking with dry sobs. Then they stood up, still silent, and stared together, hand in hand, at the trail of obliteration and destruction, which wound out of the forest and into it again. They went back, hand in hand, without looking behind them, afraid that the wicket-gate, the lawn, the stone steps, the balustrade, the terrace and the great house would be transmogrified, or simply not there. But the boys were still playing football on the lawn, a group of girls were skipping and singing shrilly on the gravel. They let go each other's hand, and went back in.

They did not speak to each other again.

The next day they were separated and placed with strange families. Their time in these families—Primrose was in a dairy farm, Penny was in a parsonage—did not in fact last very long, though then the time seemed slow-motion and endless. These alien families seemed like dream worlds into which they had strayed, not knowing the physical or social rules which constructed those worlds. Afterwards, if they remembered the evacuation it was as dreams are remembered, with mnemonics designed to claw back what fleets on waking. So Primrose remembered the sound of milk spurting in the pail, and Penny remembered the empty corsets of the vicar's wife, hanging bony on the line. They remembered dandelion clocks, but you can remember those from anywhere, any time. They remembered the thing they had seen in the forest, on the contrary, in the way you remember those very few dreams—almost all nightmares—which have the quality of life itself, not of fantasm, or shifting provisional scene-set. (Though what are dreams if not life itself?) They remembered too solid flesh, too precise a stink, a rattle and a soughing which thrilled the nerves and the cartilage of their growing ears. In the memory, as in such a dream, they felt, I cannot get out, this is a real thing in a real place.

They returned from evacuation, like many evacuees, so early that they then lived through wartime in the city, bombardment, blitz, unearthly light and roaring, changed landscapes, holes in their world where the newly dead had been. Both lost their fathers. Primrose's father was in the Army, and was killed, very late in the war, on a crowded troop-carrier sunk in the Far East. Penny's father, a much older man, was in the Auxiliary Fire Service, and died in a sheet of flame in the East India Docks on the Thames, pumping evaporating water from a puny coil of hose. They found it hard, after the war, to remember these different men. The claspers of memory could not grip the drowned and the burned. Primrose saw an inane grin under a khaki cap, because her mother had a snapshot. Penny thought she remembered her father, already grey-headed, brushing ash off his boots and trouser-cuffs as he put on his tin hat to go out. She thought she remembered a quaver of fear in his tired face, and the muscles composing themselves into resolution. It was not much, what either of them remembered.

After the war, their fates were still similar and dissimilar. Penny's widowed mother embraced grief, closed her face and her curtains, moved stiffly, like an automat, and read poetry. Primrose's mother married one of the many admirers, visitors, dancing partners she had had before the ship went down, gave birth to another five children, and developed varicose veins and a smoker's cough. She dyed her blonde hair with peroxide when it faded. Both Primrose and Penny were only children who now, because of the war, lived in amputated or unreal families. Penny developed crushes on poetical teachers and in due course—she was clever—went to university, where she chose to study developmental psychology. Primrose had little education. She was always being kept off school to look after the others. She too dyed her blonde curls with peroxide when they turned mousy and faded. She got fat as Penny got thin. Neither of them married. Penny became a child psychologist, working with the abused, the displaced, the disturbed. Primrose did this and that. She was a barmaid. She worked in a shop. She went to help at various church crèches and Salvation Army reunions, and discovered she had a talent for storytelling. She became Aunty Primrose, with her own repertoire. She was employed to tell tales to kindergartens and entertain at children's parties. She was much in demand at Hallowe'en, and had her own circle of bright yellow plastic chairs in a local shopping mall, where she kept an eye on the children of burdened women, keeping them safe, offering them just a *frisson* of fear and terror that made them wriggle with pleasure.

The house aged differently. During this period of time— whilst the little girls became women—it was handed over to the Nation, which turned it into a living museum, still inhabited by the flesh and blood descendants of those who had built it, demolished it, flung out a wing, closed off a corridor. Guided tours took place in it, at regulated times. During these tours, the ballroom and intimate drawing-rooms were fenced off with crimson twisted ropes on little brass one-eyed pedestals. The bored and the curious peered in at four-poster beds and pink silk *fauteuils*, at silver-framed photographs of wartime Royalty, and crackling crazing Renaissance and Enlightenment portraits of long-dead queens and solemn or sweetly musing ancestors. In the room where the evacuees had eaten their rationed meals, the history of the house was displayed, on posters, in glass cases, with helpful notices, and opened copies of old diaries and records. There were reproductions of the famous paintings which had lain here in hiding during the war. There was a plaque to the dead of the house: a gardener, an undergardener, a chauffeur and a second son. There were photographs of military hospital beds, and of nurses pushing wheelchairs in the grounds. There was no mention of the evacuees whose presence appeared to have been too brief to have left any trace.

The two women met in this room on an autumn day in 1984. They had come with a group, walking in a chattering crocodile behind a guide, and had lingered amongst the imagery and records, rather than going on to eavesdrop on the absent ladies and gentlemen whose tidy clutter lay on coffee tables and escritoires. They prowled around the room, each alone with herself, in opposite directions, without acknowledging each other's presence. Both their mothers had died that spring, within a week of each other, though this coincidence was unknown to them. It had made both of them think of taking a holiday, and both had chosen that part of the world. Penny was wearing a charcoal trouser suit and a black velvet hat. Primrose wore a floral knit long jacket over a shell-pink cashmere sweater, over a rustling long skirt with an elastic waist, in a mustard-coloured tapestry print. Her hips and bosom were bulky. They coincided because both of them, at the same moment, half saw an image in a medieval-looking illustrated book. Primrose thought it was a very old book. Penny assumed it was nineteenth-century mock-medieval. It showed a knight, on foot, in a forest, lifting his sword to slay something. The knight shone on the rounded slope of the page, in the light, which caught the gilding on his helmet and sword-belt. It was not possible to see what was being slain. This was because, both in the tangled vegetation of the image, and in the way the book was displayed in the case, the enemy, or victim, was in shadows.

Neither of them could read the ancient (or pseudo-ancient) black letter of the text beside the illustration. There was a typed explanation, or description, under the book, done with a faded ribbon and uneven pressure of the keys. They had to lean forward to read it, and to see what was worming its way into, or out of, the deep spine of the book, and that was how they came to see each other's face, close up, in the glass which was both transparent and reflective. Their transparent reflected faces lost detail—cracked lipstick, pouches, fine lines of wrinkles—and looked both younger and greyer, less substantial. And that is how they came to recognise each other, as they might not have done, plump face to bony face. They breathed each other's names, Penny, Primrose, and their breath misted the glass, obscuring the knight and his opponent. I could have died, I could have wet my knickers, said Penny and Primrose afterwards to each other, and both experienced this still moment as pure, dangerous shock. But they stayed there, bent heads together, legs trembling, knees knocking, and read the caption, which was about the Loathly Worm, which, tradition held, had infested the countryside and had been killed more than once by scions of that house, Sir Lionel, Sir Boris, Sir Guillem. The Worm, the typewriter had tapped out, was an English Worm, not a European dragon, and like most such worms, was wingless. In some sightings it was reported as having vestigial legs, hands or feet. In others it was limbless. It had, in monstrous form, the capacity of common or garden worms to sprout new heads or trunks if it was divided, so that two worms, or more, replaced one. This was why it had been killed so often, yet reappeared. It had been reported travelling with a slithering pack of young ones, but these may have been only revitalised segments. The typed paper was held down with drawing-pins and appeared to continue somewhere else, on some not visible page, not presented for viewing.

Being English, the recourse they thought of was tea. There was a tea-room near the great house, in a converted stable at the back. There they stood silently side by side, clutching floral plastic trays spread with briar roses, and purchased scones, superior raspberry jam in tiny jam jars, little plastic tubs of clotted cream. "You couldn't get cream or real jam in the war," said Primrose in an undertone as they found a corner table. She said wartime rationing had made her permanently greedy, and thin Penny agreed, it had, clotted cream was still a treat.

They watched each other warily, offering bland snippets of autobiography in politely hushed voices. Primrose thought Penny looked gaunt, and Penny thought Primrose

looked raddled. They established the skein of coinci-
dences—dead fathers, unmarried status, child-caring pro-
fessions, recently dead mothers. Circling like beaters, they
approached the covert thing in the forest. They discussed
the great house, politely. Primrose admired the quality of
the carpets. Penny said it was nice to see the old pictures
back on the wall. Primrose said, funny really, that there was
all that history, but no sign that they, the children, that was,
had ever been there. Penny said no, the story of the family
was there, and the wounded soldiers, but not them, they
were perhaps too insignificant. Too little, said Primrose,
nodding agreement, not quite sure what she meant by too
little. Funny, said Penny, that they should meet each other
next to that book, with that picture. Creepy, said Primrose
in a light, light cobweb voice, not looking at Penny. We saw
that thing. When we went in the forest.

Yes we did, said Penny. We saw it.

Did you ever wonder, asked Primrose, if we *really* saw it?

Never for a moment, said Penny. That is, I don't know
what it was, but I've always been quite sure we saw it.

Does it change—do you remember all of it?

It was a horrible thing, and yes, I remember all of it,
there isn't a bit of it I can manage to forget. Though I forget all sorts of things, said Penny, in a thin voice, a vanishing voice.

And have you ever told anyone of it, spoken of it, asked
Primrose more urgently, leaning forward, holding on to
the table edge.

No, said Penny. She had not. She said, who would believe it, believe them?

That's what I thought, said Primrose. I didn't speak. But it stuck in my mind like a tapeworm in your gut. I think it did me no good.

It did me no good either, said Penny. No good at all. I've thought about it, she said to the ageing woman opposite, whose face quivered under her dyed goldilocks. I think, I think there are things that are real—more real than we are—but mostly we don't cross their paths, or they don't cross ours. Maybe at very bad times we get into their world, or notice what they are doing in ours.

Primrose nodded energetically. She looked as though sharing was solace, and Penny, to whom it was not solace, grimaced with pain.

"Sometimes I think that thing finished me off," said Penny to Primrose, a child's voice rising in a woman's gullet, arousing a little girl's scared smile which wasn't a smile on Primrose's face. Primrose said:

"It did finish *her* off, that little one, didn't it? She got into its path, didn't she? And when it had gone by—she wasn't anywhere," said Primrose. "That was how it was?"

"Nobody ever asked where she was, or looked for her," said Penny.

"I wondered if we'd made her up," said Primrose. "But I didn't, we didn't."

"Her name was Alys."

"With a *y*."

There had been a mess, a disgusting mess, they remembered, but no particular sign of anything that might have
been, or been part of, or belonged to, a persistent little girl
called Alys.

Primrose shrugged voluptuously, let out a gale of a sigh,
and rearranged her flesh in her clothes.

"Well, we now know we're not mad, anyway," she said.
"We've got into a mystery, but we didn't make it up. It
wasn't a delusion. So it was good we met, because now we
needn't be afraid we're mad, need we, we can get on with
things, so to speak?"

They arranged to have dinner together the following
evening. They were staying in different bed-and-breakfasts
and neither of them thought of exchanging addresses.
They agreed on a restaurant in the market square of the
local town—*Seraphina's Hot Pot*—and a time, seven-thirty.
They did not even discuss spending the next day together.
Primrose went on a local bus tour. Penny asked for sand-
wiches, and took a long solitary walk. The weather was
grey, spitting fine rain. Both arrived at their lodgings with
headaches, and both made tea with the teabags and kettle
provided in their rooms. They sat on their beds. Penny's
bed had a quilt with blowsy cabbage roses. Primrose's had a
black-and-white checked gingham duvet. They turned on
their televisions, watched the same game show, listened to
the inordinate jolly laughter. Penny washed herself rather

fiercely in her tiny bathroom: Primrose slowly changed her underwear, and put on fresh tights. Between bathroom and wardrobe Penny saw the air in the room fill with a kind of grey smoke. Rummaging in a suitcase for a clean blouse, Primrose felt giddy, as though the carpet was swirling. What would they say to each other, they asked themselves, and sat down, heavy and winded, on the edges of their single beds. Why? Primrose's mind said, scurrying, and Why? Penny asked herself starkly. Primrose put down her blouse and turned up the television. Penny managed to walk as far as the window. She had a view with a romantic bit of moorland, rising to a height that cut off the sky. Evening had caught her: the earth was black: the house-lights trickled feebly into gloom.

Seven-thirty came and went, and neither woman moved. Both, indistinctly, imagined the other waiting at a table, watching a door open and shut. Neither moved. What could they have said, they asked themselves, but only perfunctorily. They were used to not asking too much, they had had practice.

The next day they both thought very hard, but indirectly, about the wood. It was a spring day, a good day for woods, and yesterday's rain-clouds had been succeeded by clear sunlight, with a light movement of air and a very faint warmth. Penny thought about the wood, put on her walking-shoes, and set off obliquely in the opposite direction. Primrose was not given to ratiocination. She sat over her breakfast, which was English and ample, bacon and mushrooms, toast and honey, and let her feelings about the wood run over her skin, pricking and twitching. The wood, the real and imagined wood—both before and after she had entered it with Penny—had always been simultaneously a source of attraction and a source of discomfort, shading into terror. The light in woods was more golden and more darkly shadowed than any light on city terraces, including the glare of bombardment. The gold and the shadows were intertwined, a promise of liveliness. What they had seen had been shapeless and stinking, but the wood persisted.

So without speaking to herself a sentence in her head— "I shall go there"—Primrose decided by settling her stomach, setting her knees, and slightly clenching her fists, that she would go there. And she went straight there, full of warm food, arriving as the morning brightened with the first bus-load of tourists, and giving them the slip, to take the path they had once taken, across the lawn and through the wicket-gate.

The wood was much the same, but denser and more inviting in its new greenness. Primrose's body decided to set off in a rather different direction from the one the little girls had taken. New bracken was uncoiling with snaky force. Yesterday's rain still glittered on limp new hazel leaves and threads of gossamer. Small feathered throats above her, and in the depths beyond, whistled and trilled with enchanting territorial aggression and male self-assertion, which were to Primrose simply the chorus. She heard a cackle and saw a flash of the loveliest flesh-pink, in feathers, and a blue gleam. She was not good at identifying birds. She could do "a robin"—one hopped from branch to branch—"a black bird" which shone like jet, and "a tit" which did acrobatics, soft, blue and yellow, a tiny scrap of fierce life. She went steadily on, always distracted by shines and gleams in her eye-corner. She found a mossy bank, on which she found posies of primroses, which she recognised and took vaguely, in the warmth of her heart labouring in her chest, as a good sign, a personal sign. She picked a few, stroked their pale petals, buried her nose in them, smelled the thin, clear honey-smell of them, spring honey without the buzz of summer. She was better at flowers than birds, because there had been *Flower Fairies* in the school bookshelves when she was little, with the flowers painted accurately, wood-sorrel and stitchwort, pimpernel and honeysuckle, flowers she had never seen, accompanied by truly pretty human creatures, all children, from babies to girls and boys, clothed in the blues and golds, russets and purples of the flowers and fruits, walking, dancing, delicate material imaginings of the essential lives of plants. And now as she wandered on, she saw and recognised them, windflower and bryony, self-heal and dead-nettle, and had—despite where she was—a lovely lapping sense of invisible—*just* invisible life swarming in the leaves and along the twigs, despite where she was, despite what she had not forgotten having seen there. She closed her eyes a fraction. The sunlight flickered and flickered. She saw glitter and spangling everywhere. She saw drifts of intense blue, further in, and between the tree-trunks, with the light running over them.

She stopped. She did not like the sound of her own toiling breath. She was not very fit. She saw, then, a whisking in the bracken, a twirl of fur, thin and flaming, quivering on a tree-trunk. She saw a squirrel, a red squirrel, watching her from a bough. She had to sit down, as she remembered her mother. She sat on a hummock of grass, rather heavily. She remembered them all, Nutkin and Moldywarp, Brock and Sleepy Dormous, Natty Newt and Ferdy Frog. Her mother didn't tell stories and didn't open gates into imaginary worlds. But she had been good with her fingers. Every Christmas during the war, when toys, and indeed materials, were not to be had, Primrose had woken to find in her stocking a new stuffed creature, made from fur fabric with button eyes and horny claws, or, in the case of the amphibians, made from scraps of satin and taffeta. There had been an artistry to them. The stuffed squirrel was the essence of squirrel, the fox was watchful, the newt was slithery. They did not wear anthropomorphic jackets or caps, which made it easier to invest them with imaginary natures. She believed in Father Christmas, and the discovery that her mother had made the toys, the vanishing of magic, had been a breathtaking blow. She could not be grateful for the skill and the imagination, so uncharacteristic of her flirtatious mother. The creatures continued to accumulate. A spider, a Bambi. She told herself stories at night about a girl-woman, an enchantress in a fairy wood, loved and protected by an army of wise and gentle animals. She slept banked in by stuffed creatures, as the house in the blitz was banked in by inadequate sandbags.

Primrose registered the red squirrel as disappointing—stringier and more rat-like than its plump grey city cousins. But she knew it was rare and special, and when it took off from branch to branch, flicking its extended tail like a sail, gripping with its tiny hands, she set out to follow it as though it was a messenger. It would take her to the centre, she thought, she ought to get to the centre. It could easily have leaped out of sight, she thought, but it didn't. It lingered and sniffed and stared nervily, waiting for her. She pushed through brambles into denser greener shadows. Juices stained her skirts and skin. She began to tell herself a story about staunch Primrose, not giving up, making her way to "the centre." She had to have a reason for coming there, it was to do with getting to the centre. Her childhood stories had all been in the third person. "She was not afraid." "She faced up to the wild beasts. They cowered." She laddered her tights and muddied her shoes and breathed heavier. The squirrel stopped to clean its face. She crushed bluebells and saw the sinister hoods of arum lilies.

She had no idea where she was, or how far she had come, but she decided that the clearing where she found herself was the centre. The squirrel had stopped, and was running up and down a single tree. There was a sort of mossy mound which could almost have had a throne-like aspect, if you were being imaginative. So she sat on it. "She came to the centre and sat on the mossy chair."

Now what?

She had not forgotten what they had seen, the blank miserable face, the powerful claws, the raggle-taggle train of accumulated decay. She had come neither to look for it nor to confront it, but she had come because it was there. She had known all her life that she, Primrose, had *really* been in a magic forest. She knew that the forest was the source of terror. She had never frightened the littl'uns she entertained at parties, in schools, in crèches, with tales of lost children in forests. She frightened them with slimy things that came up the plughole, or swarmed out of the U-bend in the lavatory, or tapped on windows at night, and were despatched by bravery and magic. There were waiting hobgoblins in urban dumps beyond the street-lights. But the woods in her tales were sources of glamour, of rich colours and unseen hidden life, flower fairies and more magical beings. They were places where you used words like spangles and sequins for real dewdrops on real dock leaves. Primrose knew that glamour and the thing they had seen came from the same place, that brilliance and the ashen stink had the same source. She made them safe for the littl'uns by restricting them to pantomime flats and sweet illustrations. She didn't look at what she knew, better not, but *she did know she knew*, she recognised confusedly.

Now what?

She sat on the moss, and a voice in her head said, "I

want to go home." And she heard herself give a bitter, entirely grown-up little laugh, for what was home? What did she know about home?

Where she lived was above a Chinese takeaway. She had a dangerous cupboard-corner she cooked in, a bed, a clothes-rail, an armchair deformed by generations of bottoms. She thought of this place in faded browns and beiges, seen through drifting coils of Chinese cooking-steam, scented with stewing pork and a bubbling chicken broth. Home was not real, as all the sturdy twigs and roots in the wood were real, it had neither primrose-honey nor spangles and sequins. The stuffed animals, or some of them, were piled on the bed and the carpet, their fur rubbed, their pristine stare gone from their scratched eyes. She thought about what one thought was *real*, sitting there on the moss-throne at the centre. When Mum had come in, snivelling, to say Dad was dead, she herself had been preoccupied with whether pudding would be tapioca or semolina, whether there would be jam, and subsequently, how ugly Mum's dripping nose looked, how she looked as though she was *putting it on*. She remembered the semolina and the rather nasty blackberry jam, the taste and the texture, to this day, so was that real, was that home? She had later invented a picture of a cloudy aquamarine sea under a gold sun in which a huge fountain of white curling water rose from a foundering ship. It was very beautiful but not real. She could not remember Dad. She could remember the Thing in the Forest, and she could remember Alys. The fact that the mossy tump had lovely colours—crimson and emerald, she said, maidenhairs, she named something at random—didn't mean she didn't remember the Thing. She remembered what Penny had said about "things that are more real than we are." She had met one. Here at the centre, the spout of water was more real than the semolina, because she was where such things reign. The word she found was "reign." She had understood something, and did not know what she had understood. She wanted badly to go home, and she wanted never to move. The light was lovely in the leaves. The squirrel flirted its tail and suddenly set off again, springing into the branches. The woman lumbered to her feet and licked the bramble-scratches on the back of her hands.

Penny had set off in what she supposed to be the opposite direction. She walked very steadily, keeping to hedgerows and field-edge paths, climbing the occasional stile. For the first part of the walk she kept her eyes on the ground, and her ears on her own trudging, as it disturbed stubble and pebbles. She slurred her feet over vetch and stitchwort, looking back over the crushed trail. She remembered the Thing. She remembered it clearly and daily. Why was she in this part of the world at all, if not to settle with it? But she walked away, noticing and not noticing that her path was deflected by fieldforms and the lie of the land into a snaking sickle-shape. As the day wore on, she settled into her stride and lifted her eyes, admiring the new corn in the furrows, a distant skylark. When she saw the wood on the horizon she knew it was the wood, although she was seeing it from an unfamiliar aspect, from where it appeared to be perched on a conical hillock, ridged as though it had been grasped and squeezed by coils of strength. The trees were tufted and tempting. It was almost dusk when she came there. The shadows were thickening, the dark places in the tumbled undergrowth were darkening. She mounted the slope, and went in over a suddenly discovered stile.

Once inside, she moved cautiously, as though she was hunted or hunting. She stood stock-still, and snuffed the air for the remembered rottenness: she listened to the sounds of the trees and the creatures, trying to sift out a distant threshing and sliding. She smelled rottenness, but it was normal rottenness, leaves and stems mulching back into earth. She heard sounds. Not birdsong, for it was too late in the day, but the odd raucous warning croak, a crackle of something, a tremulous shiver of something else. She heard her own heartbeat in the thickening brown air.

She had wagered on freedom and walked away, and walking away had brought her here, as she had known it would. It was no use looking for familiar tree-trunks or tussocks. They had had a lifetime, her lifetime, to alter out of recognition.

She began to think she discerned dark tunnels in the undergrowth, where something might have rolled and slid. Mashed seedlings, broken twigs and fronds, none of it very recent. There were things caught in the thorns, flimsy colourless shreds of damp wool or fur. She peered down the tunnels and noted where the scrapings hung thickest. She forced herself to go into the dark, stooping, occasionally crawling on hands and knees. The silence was heavy. She found things she remembered, threadworms of knitting wool, unravelled dishcloth cotton, clinging newsprint. She found odd sausage-shaped tubes of membrane, containing fragments of hair and bone and other inanimate stuffs. They were like monstrous owl-pellets, or the gut-shaped hair-balls vomited by cats. Penny went forwards, putting aside lashing briars and tough stems with careful fingers. It had been here, but how long ago? When she stopped, and sniffed the air, and listened, there was nothing but the drowsy wood.

Quite suddenly she came out at a place she remembered. The clearing was larger, the tree-trunks were thicker, but the fallen one behind which they had hidden still lay there. The place was almost the ghost of a camp. The trees round about were hung with threadbare pennants and streamers, like the scorched, hacked, threadbare banners in the chapel of the great house, with their brown stains of earth or blood. It had been here, it had never gone away.

Penny moved slowly and dreamily round, watching herself as you watch yourself in a dream, looking for things. She found a mock tortoiseshell hairslide, and a shoe-button with a metal shank. She found a bird-skeleton, quite fresh, bashed flat, with a few feathers glued to it. She found ambivalent shards and several teeth, of varying sizes and shapes. She found—spread around, half-hidden by roots, stained green but glinting white—a collection of small bones, fingerbones, tiny toes, a rib, and finally what might be a brain-pan and brow. She thought of putting them in her knapsack, and then thought she could not, and heaped them at the foot of a holly. She was not an anatomist. Some at least of the tiny bones might have been badger or fox.

She sat down on the earth, with her back against the fallen trunk. She thought that she should perhaps find something to dig a hole, to bury the little bones, but she didn't move. She thought, now I am watching myself as you do in a safe dream, but then, when I saw it, it was one of those appalling dreams, where you are inside, where you cannot get out. Except that it wasn't a dream.

It was the encounter with the Thing that had led her to deal professionally in dreams. Something which resembled unreality had walked—had rolled, had wound itself, had *lumbered* into reality, and she had seen it. She had been the reading child, but after the sight of the Thing, she had not been able to inhabit the customary and charming unreality of books. She had become good at studying what could not be seen. She took an interest in the dead, who inhabited real history. She was drawn to the invisible forces which moved in molecules and caused them to coagulate or dissipate. She had become a psychotherapist "to be use-ful." That was not quite accurate or sufficient as an explana-tion. The corner of the blanket that covered the unthinkable had been turned back enough for her to catch sight of it. She was in its world. It was not by accident that she had come to specialise in severely autistic children, children who twittered, or banged, or stared, who sat damp and absent on Penny's official lap and told her no dreams, dis-cussed no projects. The world they knew was a real world. Often Penny thought it was *the* real world, from which even their desperate parents were at least partly shielded. Somebody had to occupy themselves with the hopeless. Penny felt she could. Most people couldn't. She could.

All the leaves of the forest began slowly to quaver and then to clatter. Far away there was the sound of something heavy, and sluggish, stirring. Penny sat very still and expec-tant. She heard the old blind rumble, she sniffed the old stink. It came from no direction; it was on both sides; it was all around; as though the Thing encompassed the wood, or as though it travelled in multiple fragments, as it was described in the old text. It was dark now. What was visible had no distinct colour, only shades of ink and elephant.

Now, thought Penny, and just as suddenly as it had begun, the turmoil ceased. It was as though the Thing had turned away; she could feel the tremble of the wood recede and become still. Quite suddenly, over the tree-tops, a huge disc of white-gold mounted and hung, deepening shadows, silvering edges. Penny remembered her father, standing in the cold light of the full moon, and saying wryly that the bombers would likely come tonight, there was a brilliant, cloudless full moon. He had vanished in an oven of red-yellow roaring, Penny had guessed, or been told, or imagined. Her mother had sent her away before allowing the fireman to speak, who had come with the news. She had been a creep-mouse on stairs and in cubby-holes, trying to overhear what was being imparted, to be given a fragment of reality with which to attach herself to the truth of her mother's pain. Her mother didn't, or couldn't, want her company. She caught odd phrases of talk—"nothing really to identify," "absolutely no doubt." He had been a tired gentle man with ash in his trouser turn-ups. There had been a funeral. Penny remembered thinking there was nothing, or next to nothing, in the coffin his fellow-firemen shouldered, it went up so lightly, it was so easy to set down on the crematorium slab.

They had been living behind the black-out anyway, but her mother went on living behind drawn curtains long after the war was over.

She remembered someone inviting her to tea, to cheer her up. There had been indoor fireworks, saved from before the war. Chinese, set off in saucers. There had been a small conical Vesuvius, with a blue touch-paper and a pink and grey dragon painted on. It had done nothing but sputter until they had almost stopped looking, and then it spewed a coil of fantastically light ash, that rose and rose, becoming five or six times as large as the original, and then abruptly was still. Like a grey bun, or a very old turd. She began to cry. It was ungrateful of her. An effort had been made, to which she had not responded.

The moon had released the wood, it seemed. Penny stood up and brushed leaf mould off her clothes. She had been ready for it and it had not come. She did not know if she had wanted to defy it, or to see that it was as she had darkly remembered it; she felt obscurely disappointed to be released from the wood. But she accepted her release and found her way back to the fields and her village along liquid trails of moonlight.

The two women took the same train back to the city, but did not encounter each other until they got out. The passengers scurried and shuffled towards the exit, mostly heads down. Both women remembered how they had set out in the wartime dark, with their twig-legs and gasmasks. Both raised their heads as they neared the barrier, not in hope of being met, for they would not be, but automatically, to calculate where to go, and what to do. They saw each other's face in the cavernous gloom, two pale, recognisable rounds, far enough apart for speech, and even greetings, to be awkward. In the dimness they were reduced to similarity—dark eyeholes, set mouth. For a moment or two, they stood and simply stared. On that first occasion the station vault had been full of curling steam, and the air gritty with ash. Now, the blunt-nosed sleek diesel they had left was blue and gold under a layer of grime. They saw each other through that black imagined veil which grief, or pain, or despair hang over the visible world. They saw each other's face and thought of the unforgettable misery of the face they had seen in the forest. Each thought that the other was the witness, who made the thing certainly real, who prevented her from slipping into the comfort of believing she had imagined it, or made it up. So they stared at each other, blankly and desperately, without acknowledgement, then picked up their baggage, and turned away into the crowd.

Penny found that the black veil had somehow become part of her vision. She thought constantly about faces, her father's, her mother's—neither of which would hold their form in her mind's eye. Primrose's face, the hopeful little girl, the woman staring up at her from the glass case, staring at her conspiratorially over the clotted cream. The blonde infant Alys, an ingratiating sweet smile. The half-human face of the Thing. She tried, as though everything depended on it, to remember that face completely, and suffered over the detail of the dreadful droop of its mouth, the exact inanity of its blind squinneying. Present faces were blank discs, shadowed moons. Her patients came and went, children lost, or busy, or trapped behind their masks of vagueness or anxiety or over-excitement. She was increasingly unable to distinguish one from another. The face of the Thing hung in her brain, jealously soliciting her attention, distracting her from dailiness. She had gone back to its place, and had not seen it. She needed to see it. Why she needed it, was because it was more real than she was. It would have been better not even to have glimpsed it, but their paths had crossed. It had trampled on her life, had sucked out her marrow, without noticing who or what she was. She would go and face it. What else was there, she asked herself, and answered herself, nothing.

So she made her way back, sitting alone in the train as the fields streaked past, drowsing through a century-long night under the cabbage-rose quilt in the B&B. This time she went in the old way, from the house, through the garden-gate; she found the old trail quickly, her sharp eye picked up the trace of its detritus, and soon enough she was back in the clearing, where her cairn of tiny bones by the tree-trunk was undisturbed. She gave a little sigh, dropped to her knees, and then sat with her back to the rotting wood and silently called the Thing. Almost immediately she sensed its perturbation, saw the trouble in the branches, heard the lumbering, smelled its ancient smell. It was a greyish, unre-markable day. She closed her eyes briefly as the noise and movement grew stronger. When it came, she would look it in the face, she would see what it was. She clasped her hands loosely in her lap. Her nerves relaxed. Her blood slowed. She was ready.

Primrose was in the shopping mall, putting out her circle of rainbow-coloured plastic chairs. She creaked as she bent over them. It was pouring with rain outside, but the mall was enclosed like a crystal palace in a casing of glass. The floor under the rainbow chairs was gleaming dappled marble. They were in front of a dimpling fountain, with lights shining up through the greenish water, making golden rings round the polished pebbles and wishing-coins that lay there. The little children collected round her: their mothers kissed them good-bye, told them to be good and quiet and listen to the nice lady. They had little transparent plastic cups of shining orange juice, and each had a biscuit in silver foil. They were all colours—black skin, brown skin, pink skin, freckled skin, pink jacket, yellow jacket, purple hood, scarlet hood. Some grinned and some whimpered, some wriggled, some were still. Primrose sat on the edge of the fountain. She had decided what to do. She smiled her best, most comfortable smile, and adjusted her golden locks. Listen to me, she told them, and I'll tell you something amazing, a story that's never been told before.

There were once two little girls who saw, or believed they saw, a thing in a forest . . .

Angels & Insects
TWO NOVELLAS

In "Morpho Eugenia," a shipwrecked naturalist is rescued by a family whose clandestine passions come to seem as inscrutable as the behavior of insects. In "The Conjugial Angel," a circle of fictional mediums finds itself haunted by the ghost of a historical personage.
Fiction/Literature/0-679-75134-3

Babel Tower

At the heart of *Babel Tower* are two law cases, twin strands of the Establishment's web, which shape the story: a painful divorce and custody suit and the prosecution of an "obscene" book. Frederica, the independent young heroine, is involved in both. The resulting tale, charted with a brilliant imaginative sympathy, is as comic as it is threatening and bizarre.
Fiction/Literature/0-679-73680-8

The Biographer's Tale

Phineas G. Nanson is a disenchanted graduate student who decides to escape the world of postmodern literary theory and immerse himself in the messiness of "real life" by writing a biography of a great biographer. In a series of adventures that are by turns intellectual and comic, scientific and sensual, Phineas tracks his subject to the deserts of Africa and the maelstroms of the Arctic.
Fiction/Literature/0-375-72508-3

The Djinn in the Nightingale's Eye

The magnificent title story of this collection of fairy tales for adults describes the strange and uncanny relationship between its extravagantly intelligent heroine—a world-renowned scholar of the art of storytelling—and the marvelous being that lives in a mysterious bottle, found in a dusty shop in an Istanbul bazaar. This collection of stories draws us into narratives that are as mesmerizing as dreams and as bracing as philosophical meditations.

Fiction/Literature/0-679-76222-1

Elementals

A beautiful ice maiden risks her life when she falls in love with a desert prince. A woman flees the scene of her husband's heart attack. And a wealthy Englishwoman gradually loses her identity while wandering through a shopping mall. This richly imaginative story collection transports the reader to a world where opposites clash and converge.

Fiction/Literature/0-375-70575-9

The Game

A story of two sisters, Cassandra and Julia, once close, but now hostile strangers. Confronted by a man from their past, who they once both loved and suffered over, they struggle with each other toward a denouement that is both shocking and as inevitable as a classical tragedy.

Fiction/Literature/0-679-74256-5

Imagining Characters (with Ignês Sodré)

In this innovative and wide-ranging book, Byatt and the psychoanalyst Ignês Sodré bring their different sensibilities to bear on six novels they have read and loved: Jane Austen's *Mansfield*

Park, Charlotte Brönte's *Villette,* George Elliot's *Daniel Deronda,* Willa Cather's *The Professor's House,* Iris Murdoch's *An Unofficial Rose,* and Toni Morrison's *Beloved.* The results are nothing less than an education in the ways literature grips its readers and, at times, transforms their lives.
Psychology/Literature/0-679-77753-9

Little Black Book of Stories

Two middle-aged women walk into a forest, as they did when they were girls, confronting the strange thing they saw—or thought they saw—so long ago. A distinguished male obstetrician and a young woman artist meet in a hospital. A man meets the ghost of his living wife; a woman turns to stone. And an innocent member of an evening creative writing class turns out to have her own decided views on the best way to use "raw material." These unforgettable stories are by turns haunting, funny, sparkling, and scary.
Fiction/Literature/1-4000-7560-2

The Matisse Stories

An elegant collection of three intensely observed, beatifully written stories, each inspired by a painting by Henri Matisse, each revealing the intimate connection between seeing and feeling.
Fiction/Literature/0-679-76223-X

Passions of the Mind

Thoughtfully and stylishly, A. S. Byatt considers the parallels between George Eliot and Willa Cather; Robert Browning's spiritual malaise and the mythic strands in the novels of Saul Bellow and Iris Murdoch; and other matters of art and intellect both past and present.
Literary Criticism/Literature/0-679-73678-6

Possession

Winner of England's Booker Prize and a literary sensation, *Possession* is both an exhilarating intellectual mystery and a triumphant love story of a pair of young scholars researching the lives of two Victorian poets.

Fiction/Literature/0-679-73590-9

Sugar and Other Stories

This dazzling collection of short fiction explores the fragile ties between generations, the dizzying abyss of loss, and the elaborate memories we construct against it.

Fiction/Literature/0-679-74227-1

The Virgin in the Garden

A wonderfully erudite entertainment about a brilliant and eccentric family in which enlightenment and sexuality, Elizabethan drama and contemporary comedy intersect richly and unpredictably.

Fiction/Literature/0-679-73829-0

A Whistling Woman

Frederica Potter lucks into a job hosting a groundbreaking television talk show based in London. Meanwhile, in her native Yorkshire where her lover is involved in academic research, the university is planning a prestigious conference on body and mind, and a group of students and agitators is establishing an Anti-University. And nearby a therapeutic community is beginning to take the shape of a religious cult. *A Whistling Woman* is a brilliant and thought-provoking meditation on psychology, science, religion, ethics, and radicalism and their effects on ordinary lives.

Fiction/Literature/0-679-77690-7